THE BILLIONAIRE'S
CHALLENGE

By Elizabeth Lennox

Chapter 1

A scowling hawk settled in among the fluttering butterflies.

Selena faltered as she pulled her gaze from the man who folded his massive frame into one of the chairs at the back of the training room. "So tell your clients *not* to drink this! External use *only*," she stressed, waiting until the laughter settled down again. "This is a serum for the skin and, trust me, after a week, you *will* notice a difference. It's amazing! Softer skin is only a few drops away!" The ladies who worked the retail counters for Rembrandt Cosmetics were frantically scribbling notes, eager to hurry back to their makeup counters at the various upscale department stores so they could sell the new products.

She moved on to the next product, explaining the value of it, application process, and any tips to help sell the product. On and on, she moved from skin care to color palettes to body products, painfully aware of the man. It would be hard to miss him since the ladies were all wearing the bright, lemon yellow smocks which were the uniforms for Rembrandt representatives. Even the training room was painted the signature color with green lettering, the chairs were lemon yellow, the desks green, the curtains green, the walls yellow.

So the man in the dark suit stood out like...well, like a scowling hawk. Ready to swoop down and grab one of the dainty ladies. None of the women noticed that the man was there. It helped that the man had stepped in silently and sat down, not saying a word.

"Okay, ladies! That's it for the day! If you have any questions, feel free to ask. I'm more than happy to clarify anything you might not understand."

The room breathed a sigh of relief. Slowly, the ladies gathered up their belongings, chatting amongst themselves. Selena would have smiled with the triumph of a job well done, but the man in the back of the room was watching her closely, which left her uneasy.

Selena gathered up her notes and packed them away, eyeing the man warily. She sensed that the man might be trying to appear laid back, but...no. He wasn't relaxed. Selena doubted that he even knew how to relax. Looking at him, she doubted that the man even slept.

Mentally, she chided herself for her ridiculous ruminations. Of course the man slept. Everyone slept! This man might just sleep... less.

As the room emptied, he approached the podium. Not good, she thought, but stiffened her wobbly self-confidence, refusing to be "that" woman. She'd forcefully banished "that" woman from her life a long time ago.

"May I help you?" she asked, leaning her head back further than she expected. Wow, he was impressively tall.

The man extended his hand. "I'm Reid Jones. You're an excellent trainer."

Selena blinked at the name, surprised and more than slightly awed. "*You're* Mr. Jones? CEO of Rembrandt Cosmetics?" she asked, a bit too breathlessly, and closed her eyes, shaking her head slightly. "I'm sorry, silly question." Opening her eyes, she took a deep breath and straightened her shoulders. "It's a pleasure to meet you, sir," she stuck her hand into his enormous one.

She was startled by the shock that sizzled through her as his fingers closed over hers, but she tried to hide it. This wasn't just a big kahuna in Rembrandt Cosmetics, the cosmetics company for which she worked. This was *THE* big kahuna! Wait, there were two of them, she thought quickly, trying to place this particular one.

"Call me Reid," he smiled, distracting her from trying to place him correctly in the corporate hierarchy.

She might have relaxed or smiled at his offer, but his hand was still holding hers and Selena couldn't seem to pull her eyes away from his hypnotic gaze. The look in his eyes...she sensed a strange expression, a look that caused her feminine instincts to stand up and take notice...but she couldn't quite define what it was.

Was it attraction?

No! Impossible!

Selena wasn't all that great in the relationships arena so she dismissed the idea, focusing on the fact that this was her boss's boss's boss's boss. This was the man in charge, the creator, founder, and director of Rembrandt Cosmetics.

"Yes. Right." Staring up into his eyes, she shivered slightly. They were the color of dark chocolate and held whispers of untold delights in their depths.

She blinked and stared at her shoes, fearing he might think she was flirting.

Not that she was! Even if she wanted to flirt, she didn't know how. Her history...the whole learning-how-to-flirt period of her life...well, that hadn't happened. She'd never learned and after... well...that one, horrible night, she'd never even bothered to try learning. So Selena accepted that flirting just wasn't...well, she couldn't do it. Not really. She looked like an idiot whenever she tried so she simply didn't try.

Swallowing a sigh, she focused back on the man, all the while trying not to focus too hard on him. He was so tall, with broad shoulders and…well, wow!

She squared her shoulders and tried to focus. This was business. This was the owner and founder of the company! His eyes seemed to promise something but she didn't want to try to interpret the message, sure that she'd mess up the translation.

"You are an excellent trainer, Ms. Bailey."

"Please, call me Selena," she replied automatically. "And thank you. I truly enjoy my job."

He chuckled softly. "Exactly what any good employee would say when confronted by the boss."

She smiled as well, feeling his soft laughter all the way down to her toes. Something curled inside of her. She should probably be flattered, but she'd learned the hard way not to wish looks from men meant something more than what they were.

"You're very kind," she realized that he was still holding her hand and pulled away. "What brings you to Virginia?" she asked, grasping for a topic. She stepped back, putting the podium and table between them. The air around him seemed to sizzle. She stared like a deer caught in headlights until he broke her trance with a smile that seemed incredibly sexy somehow.

She jumped, looking down at the papers and cosmetics scattered across the table. With shaking fingers, she clumsily started stuffing everything into her bag. Anything to distract her from the oddly intense pull drawing her towards the man.

What are you thinking, she mentally chided herself. Keep your eyes off him. Ignore those wickedly broad shoulders and that taut, tapered waist. Even though it was nice. Very nice! The whole man's body was incredibly fit and nice and…well…amazing!

"I saw your marketing ideas," he announced.

That grabbed her attention, and she dropped the lipstick she'd just picked up. Her marketing ideas? The ones she's submitted just last week? Woah!

Shock stole her voice for a long moment before she gathered her wits and straightened her shoulders. "You did?"

He smiled slightly, not a full-out smile. Nor could the flash of his expression be considered even a grin. But there was a curling of his lips and his white teeth showed for a brief moment.

"Not only did I read through your plan, but a brilliant financial analyst has already done a work up of the cost to implement your ideas. They're good, Selena. Really good!"

The blush was fast and furious, but thankfully, dissipated before she looked too foolish. "Thank you," she replied, hoping she sounded professional instead of silly and flustered.

"I flew out here to discuss it with you. Do you have plans for dinner?"

He wanted to discuss her ideas?! How crazy was that? "Dinner?"

He chuckled, making those thrilling shivers race through her body again. "Yes. Tonight, if you don't have other plans."

Darn it, that blush hit her again. Looking down, she thought about the spin class that she'd planned to take tonight. She tried to remember the gym's schedule...but the thought of spending time with this man distracted her.

One thing was certain; when the chief executive officer of one's company asked to discuss your idea over dinner, one went to dinner with said CEO!

She nodded in what she hoped was a professional manner and not a reflection of the silly, schoolgirl excitement that saturated her body. "Yes. Dinner would be perfect."

"You had plans?"

Boy, he was perceptive! Or maybe she just wasn't good at

hiding her thoughts. She waved her hand dismissively. "Nothing urgent."

"Excellent." He pushed away from the desk he'd been leaning against and she realized all over again how tall he was. "Are you ready now?"

Now? As in...this moment? She looked down at her uniform and shook her head. "Yes! Of course." She unbuttoned the lemon yellow smock with fumbling fingers while searching for her bag at the same time.

"Looking for this?"

She spun around and, sure enough, her pretty, leather tote was dangling from his fingers. Somehow, the bag actually looked delicately sexy there. He was all tough, strong, and raw while her bag was about as feminine as it could be without being pink and flowered.

"Yes," she replied, clearing her throat slightly. "Thank you."

"My pleasure." He gestured towards the doorway and she smiled nervously. With any other man, she would simply follow. But in this case, she was painfully aware of him behind her. She'd worn a simple, black sheath dress today with her favorite yellow heels, the ones that matched the Rembrandt Cosmetic's uniform perfectly. Thankfully, they gave her another three inches, additional height that she definitely needed. But her shoes suddenly seemed a bit frivolous, even though they perfectly matched the amazing necklace she'd found last week. Caressing the delicate, linked blossoms, she wondered if she looked too frivolous.

If Reid had imagined the person who had submitted the brilliant marketing suggestion, he might have pictured a woman in her fifties wearing a sleek bun at the back of her neck and dark, severe suits with bright red lipstick and a sharp look in her eye that announced she was all business. So being faced with this stunning woman, soft, silky curls cascading over slender shoulders, delicate, almost elven features, and gorgeous blue eyes, he was enchanted. Surprised, amazed, and enchanted.

"You look beautiful," he assured her when he noticed her nervously fingering the delicate yellow necklace. The movement brought his attention to her throat and Reid wondered if she was sensitive there. Or maybe along her ear? He'd already noted that she wasn't wearing a ring. Neither a wedding ring nor an engagement ring.

A good thing, because he was more than interested. Hell, he even liked the sexy heels she wore even though she'd probably break an, admittedly sexy, ankle if she had to sprint anywhere.

Startled, she glanced over her shoulder at him.

He put a hand to her elbow. "You were touching your necklace, and you seemed self-conscious. I like it. The necklace suits you."

Another blush. Damn, he liked that. He suddenly realized that the women he normally dated were tall and athletic. They wore heels, but they were more severe. This woman's shoes were... pretty. It also occurred to him that the women in his past rarely wore jewelry except for perhaps sedate, gold earrings.

This delicate butterfly was about as far as possible from the women he was normally drawn to, but he couldn't deny the instant, clawing need to...get to know her better. In many ways, he thought, as he held the door open.

The painfully hot sunshine combined with humidity that generally hovered in the seventy percent range hit both of them like a wet blanket as they stepped out of the air-conditioned office building. Virginia in the summertime was miserable. But Northern Virginia, where most of the federal government workers lived, was especially bad because, on top of the heat and humidity, one had to deal with the traffic. In a recent report, the Washington, D.C. traffic was listed as the worst in the country, even worse than Los

Angeles and New York City. Not a list one wanted to top, but the residents of this area earned it.

From June through September, the sweltering, miserable heat was more pronounced because one had to sit in almost unmoving traffic just about any time of the day or night. During the winters, God help the area if even a snowflake appeared. The drivers in this metropolitan area didn't get enough snow to learn how to drive in it. So even the smallest of snowfalls caused traffic to snarl and numerous accidents turned highways into parking lots.

Right now, the heat was in the nineties with no end in sight. Add in the seventy-plus percentage of humidity and the air felt like it was in the triple digits. Clothes stuck to one's back, naturally curly hair curled into tight spirals and naturally straight hair lost any sort of bounce, laying limp against one's neck. It was miserable!

"I don't know how you deal with summers here," he growled, taking off his jacket after only a few steps along the sidewalk.

Selena laughed and he turned his head, wanting to see those blue eyes sparkle.

"No one gets used to this kind of heat," she assured him. He put a hand to the small of her back, not because she needed assistance, but because he wanted to touch her again.

"So why don't you move? Find some place where the summers aren't a miserable marathon of humidity and dread?"

Another laugh. Reid realized he could really get used to hearing her laughter. "Well, the summers are horrible here in Virginia, but remember, Washington, D.C. was built on a swamp. So it's not surprising that the weather during July and August and...yeah, sometimes June and September...is so bad." He opened the door to a black Land Rover, gesturing for her to get in.

Before stepping into the soft leather of the SUV, she tilted her face to smile up at him and her beauty took his breath away.

His gut tightened as anticipation hit him hard. It took all of his concentration and self-discipline to hear her next words.

"Wait until autumn arrives! This area might be bad in the summer months, but in the spring and fall, the DC area is the most glorious place to live!"

And she slipped gracefully into the seat. He stood there, watching with rapt attention as she pulled her legs in. Strong legs, he noticed. He couldn't see her thighs, because her dress came down to just below her knees, but her calves were strong and lean, well muscled. Sexy as hell! Damn, she was gorgeous!

Yeah, he had a thing for legs. And her legs were...extraordinary!

But still, his reaction to her was so out of character! This sudden and intense attraction wasn't normal. Perhaps he was jaded, but while women were pretty and enjoyable, none had ever made him feel this...he wasn't sure how to describe what he was feeling. But the sudden urge to pound his chest like a caveman was ridiculous!

He looked up, realized that she was waiting for him to close the car door and smiled slightly. And yes, he glanced down at her legs one more time before he closed the door.

"What would you like to eat tonight?" he asked as he pressed the button to start the engine. He turned, sliding his arm behind her seat to look at her, noting the dilated irises and the pulse pounding at the base of her throat. Perfect! She felt it too.

"Umm...anything is fine with me."

"Thai? Mexican? Something less ethnic?" He admired her arms, bare from the shoulders, noticing even her arms were muscular. Yeah, that turned him on too.

"I love Thai!" she exclaimed, her shoulders straightening with excitement.

"Thai it is. I know of a great Thai place over in Fairfax. Well, more of a hole in the wall really. I think there are about six tables total, but it's worth it. Promise!"

Decision made, he backed the SUV out of the parking spot. If he leaned into her a bit, getting a whiff of her perfume, that wasn't a crime. It took a moment for him to recognize the scent as their signature perfume, "Rembrandt", which smelled more erotic on her than he ever would have expected! Yes, he knew that the oils and other ingredients mixed with a woman's individual body chemistry. But the spicy, feminine scent hit him hard and fast. The scent wasn't cloying, or overly sweet, like some perfumes. It was made to be light, almost airy, but with a floral scent mixed in with a bit of cinnamon and vanilla. He'd heard from other customers that they enjoyed the scent because of the different layers, but on Selena, those layers became a siren call.

Selena folded her hands in her lap, not really sure what to do. The man smelled...amazing! He smelled like fresh air, pine, and male. How was that possible? Rembrandt Cosmetics didn't sell a male product line, but sitting in the close confines of the SUV, she thought that this particular scent should definitely be bottled.

Turning slightly, Selena tried to suppress the scorching desire, reminding herself that she was a professional. "So, if you don't like Virginia in the summer time, why are you here? Is there some secret product release that we're getting soon?"

He controlled the vehicle easily and with confidence. The traffic was heavy, but he wasn't one of those arrogant drivers who cut people off in order to get ahead of one vehicle. He took the back roads, avoiding the main arteries of the Four-Ninety-Five beltway or Interstate Sixty-Six that took residents from the edge of Washington D. C. all the way out to edge of suburbia and beyond. Both of those routes would be parking lots at this time of the day. Instead, he took the less known roads.

"I came here to meet you and discuss the marketing idea you submitted," he reminded her.

"Yes, but what *else*?"

"No other reason. Brant, my brother and the chief operating officer, and I listened to our marketing director explain your ideas yesterday. I flew out today specifically to talk with you."

"You came out here just to hear about a marketing idea?"

He nodded his head. "Yes. Your idea, bolstered by the fact that sales in your district are higher than any other area in the country, confirmed the decision to come out and meet you in person. I want to hear more and understand the genesis of your ideas. They're great!"

This time, the pink in her cheeks was the flush of pride. "Thank you," she said softly, but with a sincerity that came from her heart.

"No, thank *you*. Your idea was well researched and well thought out. We get ideas all the time, but most don't have details and data to back them up." He pulled into a small strip mall, which surprised Selena. He had an underlying elegance about him that shouted "extreme wealth". He had said something about a hole in the wall restaurant, but Selena hadn't believed him.

She stepped out, shielding her eyes from the evening sun, and stared at the restaurant. It was tiny, with the tackiest décor she'd ever seen, and it seemed completely deserted. But the smells! Goodness, the scent of food made her stomach scream!

"I promise that the food here is better than the décor. I stop by whenever I'm in the area because it's really that good."

Darn it, she hoped he didn't notice the way she shivered every time he touched her. How embarrassing!

Pasting what she hoped was a confident smile on her face, she nodded. "It certainly smells amazing," she walked slightly ahead of him but stepped back when he reached around her to open the door. Wow, good looking and a gentleman! How...rare!

"Thank you," she murmured as she stepped through the door. She got another whiff of that male scent and breathed in.

"You're welcome," he replied. Had his voice gotten huskier somehow? Even his eyes seemed darker.

"Mr. Jones!" an elderly voice called. "What are you doing out in this miserable heat?" the voice demanded. A moment later, a tiny woman appeared from behind the chipped, dingy counter, her arms outstretched, wearing an enormous smile that revealed missing teeth and sparkling brown eyes. "Shouldn't you be back on your mountain, doing fun things in the nicer summer weather?"

Reid immediately hugged the tiny woman who must be the owner of the restaurant.

"Elsbeth! How have you been?"

The two of them chatted about her kids and grandchildren, before she turned her weathered eyes on Selena. "Ah! You finally bring your bride to meet me, eh?"

Selena jerked, her mouth dropping open in horror at the mistake. "No! Oh no," she gestured between Reid and herself. "We're not married!"

The woman cackled for a moment, then shook her head. "Not yet, right?"

Selena's face burned with embarrassment. "No! Oh, my goodness! Sir, I'm so sorry!" She glanced up at Reid, who looked as if he was fighting back laughter. "This is just a business dinner!"

The woman nodded. Reaching out, she patted Selena's hand. "You keep telling yourself that, dear. In the meantime," she turned slightly, "you sit here. I get you food."

Reid stepped behind one of the chairs, holding it for her. She stared at him for a long moment, surprised. It was one thing for a man to hold a door for a woman. But holding out her chair? That was a lost art. No one had ever held her chair before and she wasn't really sure what to do.

Sitting down, she glanced behind her as he pushed in her chair. She couldn't help but wonder why he was being so polite. She was just an employee. And not even one that was high up the corporate chart! In the grand scheme of her world, Selena accepted that she was one of the worker bees of this corporation. She was good at her job and loved it, but she didn't pretend that it was as important as what the employees at the headquarters out in Colorado did for the company.

"Tell me how you came up with the ideas you sent to me." He leaned forward eagerly, eyes sparkling with curiosity.

Ah, firmer ground, she thought with a sigh of relief. "Well, I flew out to your corporate headquarters in Denver last fall for a training class and noticed that most of the women there didn't wear much makeup. They went for more natural colors, but with a little flare. Whereas, when I travel downtown to Washington, D.C., I notice the women wear almost no makeup at all. In New York, the look is all about red lips and lots of color."

Reid nodded, his dark eyes flashing approval as he continued, "And in the south, Virginia included, the look is softer, more feminine. And they wear more makeup."

"Exactly! So I thought about how to market to not just the different areas of the country, but also the various groups of women. Such as the suburban mother, who might not put on makeup until the end of the day, if at all, because she's running around with her children, cleaning the house, or meeting with teachers. Or the working mother who has about five minutes to put on makeup before she has to run out the door so she can drop her kids off at school or day care, then get to that meeting someone obnoxiously scheduled at eight in the morning."

"I loved your idea about a lower cost line of products for teenagers. Where did that come from?"

Selena smiled briefly, thinking back to the day she'd thought of it. "I was getting my mail one afternoon and my neighbor's daughter was doing the same thing. We chatted for a moment, but I was so distracted by her eye makeup that I couldn't tell you what we were discussing. It was awful, clashed terribly with her skin tone, and wasn't well applied. When we started discussing makeup, she mentioned she borrowed her mother's makeup but it didn't really work for her." Selena shrugged slightly. "Then I thought about luxury car companies. Over the past decade, they started making inexpensive cars, priced for college kids who'd just started their first job. They don't have a lot of money, but they like the prestige of the brand. The car companies earn the loyalty early on with a quality, lower-cost product, and the consumers understand that there will always be a more expensive car they can exchange for when they get their next raise or promotion." She shifted slightly in her chair, excited about her idea. "That's when I came up with the idea of boxing the various products for the individual consumer based off needs. It's much easier for a busy working mom or a mother with kids to walk up to one of our counters and ask for the 'box for me' instead of trying to figure out all of the various items. I figure it will take them five minutes at the counter to figure out their skin tone and colors. From that moment forward, they need only submit something online and the box with colors and makeup is sent directly to them. Although, they don't have to buy the whole box all the time, just what they run out of. It is a way to up-sell, but with compassion for busy lifestyles."

He watched her for a long moment. Selena had trouble remaining still under his continued perusal, but finally, he nodded his head. "It's brilliant, actually. I love the idea."

Their food arrived and, although though neither of them had taken a moment to glance at the menu, the elderly woman brought out every one of Selena's favorites.

Downing a huge glass of water, she picked up chopsticks

and dug into the curry chicken and basil plate, ignoring the rice completely.

As they ate, he continued to ask questions and she warmed under his genuine appreciation for her ideas. Never had anyone paid her this kind of attention before and it was startling and gratifying.

"Have you had enough to eat?" he asked, glancing at her plate. "You hardly ate anything."

She looked down as well, noticed that he'd eaten a huge amount of food. She patted her stomach and smiled gratefully. "I'm full. Thank you. You are right, the food here is wonderful."

He stood up and pulled out his wallet. "Good. Let's get dessert."

She shook her head. "No need for dessert," she told him, thinking she needed to go for a long run in order to release the tension that had only intensified during the meal. Frustration from the almost continuous awareness of him as a man was hitting her hard and fast. A good, long run would ease some of the tension that had built up in her back and shoulders during the meal. While dessert sounded lovely, she knew that she couldn't manage all that sugar.

"There's every need for dessert," he countered. He tossed several bills down onto the table, probably twice what the actual meal costs. "Elsbeth! Everything was delicious! See you next time, okay?"

The woman appeared out from behind the curtain that guarded the secrets of the kitchen from the dining area, a huge grin splitting her features. "Next time you come back, have a ring on your woman's finger!" she admonished.

Reid. "I'll work on it," he promised.

Then he led Selena out of the restaurant. "I'm sorry about that," she told him.

He waved that away. "Don't worry about Elsbeth. She's a hopeless romantic and thinks she knows everyone's business."

Once more, he held the door open for her and waited until she'd pulled her legs inside. While she attached the seatbelt, he closed the door and walked around. "So no dessert. How about a glass of wine?" he offered. "There's more to this request than just information on how this got started."

She shrugged, liking the idea. Probably dangerous, but...why not? She hadn't had a glass of wine in...years! "Okay, there's a small pub right across from my apartment building. Would that be okay? That way I wouldn't have to take the Metro home." She cringed at how that sounded. "I mean, if it's not too much trouble, that is."

"Your apartment it is," he told her.

Another cringe. "I didn't mean to imply that I was...that *wasn't* a sexual suggestion. I don't...we aren't..."

He laughed softly. "Selena, it's much too early in our relationship for sex."

She sighed with relief, her shoulders relaxing. But then his words sank in and her whole body stiffened with...horror? Too *early* for sex? Huh? What did he mean by that? She couldn't interpret his expression.

So instead of saying anything or making a fool of herself with another silly blush, she turned to face forward while he drove towards her apartment building.

It was only a short drive to her apartment. She had him park in the space across the street where the pub was located. She could just walk across the street from there.

Once they were seated in the intimately lit interior, she realized that this suggestion had been a mistake. She ordered a glass of white wine and he asked for a beer.

Needing to return to business, she leaned forward, looking into his eyes with a determination that sprung from a deep-need inside of her to control her world. "Okay, what else do you need to know about the marketing plan?"

He gazed at her and Selena's muscles tightened with the weight of that look.

"I need to know when you're coming out to Denver to implement the plan." He watched her for a long moment before continuing. "We'll pay all your relocation costs, plus a salary increase." He named a figure. Selena gasped, not sure she'd heard him correctly. Surely, he hadn't meant that number in dollars!

"Plus you'll be flying to the various cities to train the trainers and implement the details. I estimate that it will take approximately six months to get the marketing plan in place and the materials designed. Another six months to get the publicity details worked out. Then six months to travel around to train everyone on the new concept." He waited, letting the details sink in. "How about next week?"

She stared at him, her mind trying to catch up. "Next week... what?"

He smiled slightly. "Selena, my brother and I started this company because we knew what we liked. Women, cosmetics...we knew the kind of look we wanted to go for and we accomplished that goal, building the company into a renowned international brand. We know what we like. We know what works. You're the one who thought up the idea and I want *you* to deliver it for Rembrandt Cosmetics. The idea is huge. It's a massive change in the way we've been doing things but it will definitely put us ahead of the competition. Your idea is solid, innovative, and affordable to a wide range of people. I anticipate that the appeal will be immediate and intense."

Their drinks arrived and she leaned back, allowing the waitress to set her wine in front of her, but she didn't touch it. His beer looked delicious, tall, golden, with a small bit of foam at the top. But...moving to Denver? Leaving this area?

"Are you kidding me?" she whispered, shocked and more flattered than she could believe.

"I'm completely serious."

She nodded her head, trying to think about everything he'd just said. "This is a lot to take in," she told him.

He put a hand over hers. "Why don't you think about it tonight? Write down all your concerns and we'll discuss them tomorrow morning, over breakfast. Does that sound fair?"

Selena thought about it for a long moment, then nodded her head. "Yes. Very fair."

"Good. Talk it over with your boyfriend and see what he thinks."

She shook her head, still reeling with the offer. "I don't have a boyfriend," she admitted absently.

"Good. My research says that your parents are retired, living down in Florida and you rent an apartment here, so you won't have to worry about selling your house." He lifted a hand to stop her next words. "We'll negotiate with your landlord if you're in the middle of a long term contract." He waited another moment. "Whatever the obstacle, I'll figure out how to remove it, Selena. I want you out in Denver, getting started on this project."

"Why do you need *me*?"

He smiled slightly. "I've learned that getting someone who believes in a project tends to ensure the success of that project. You believe in this idea. Furthermore, as you start working through the details, I suspect that you'll find more ways to enhance and expand further. It makes sense to move you out to Denver, so you'll be close by."

She smiled, feeling hope blossom inside of her. "Okay, I'll think about it."

"Good!"

Chapter 2

What was she thinking?! She couldn't move to Denver! It was a different world out there! Her life was here!

Selena paced back and forth across her apartment, her mind spinning with all of the questions and worries. Move to Denver... stay here. Moving to Denver would definitely be an adventure but...she *lived* here!

But really, what would she be missing? She had her gym and exercise classes, but there were gyms and classes in Denver. She had her apartment, but it was a tiny one bedroom located in Arlington, right outside of Washington, D.C. and rent was more than it should be. She'd already looked up some rentals in Denver and they were several hundred dollars cheaper.

She wasn't in love with this area. Selena had moved here simply because of the job. So there weren't any emotional ties to the area.

Besides, the salary increase was huge!

She looked around the small apartment with the tan walls and her tan love seat because the apartment was too small for a full sized couch. She wouldn't miss the miserable summers, that was for sure. Even now, it was eleven o'clock at night and it was still hot and humid.

The current temperature in Denver was a soothing seventy degrees. "It's a dry heat," she said out loud to the empty apartment. Shaking her head, she slumped down onto the love seat. "What exactly is a dry heat? And why is that so much better? What's wrong with a bit of heat and humidity? Who cares if I can't see outside of my windows some mornings because of the humidity?"

She leaned her head back against the cushions, staring up at the ceiling.

"I don't want to go because of *him*," she admitted quietly. Looking back down at her computer where she'd started building a pros and cons list, she flipped over to her Google search and skimmed through the images. He really was gorgeous in a rugged way. There was almost always a bit of scruff on his jawline. She suspected it was because the man just grew facial hair at a faster rate. There were several pictures of him in the morning sunshine and he looked freshly shaved. And a few at night wearing a tuxedo and...yep. Freshly shaved, as if he'd shaved moments before pulling on that striking tuxedo jacket.

With an exasperated huff, she slapped the laptop closed. "Why am I even hesitating? I hate the summers here! Winters aren't all that much better either and...well, they presumably have seasons in Colorado! Beautiful seasons aren't exclusive to this area."

And so it went, back and forth throughout the night. By the time morning rolled around, she was no closer to a decision.

When she stepped out of her building, the first thing she saw was Reid leaning against the Land Rover, looking incredibly gorgeous and relaxed in a pair of jeans and tee-shirt that hugged the muscular biceps she hadn't noticed before because of his suit and tailored dress shirt yesterday.

It was all a façade, she thought. Not the gorgeous part, but he definitely wasn't relaxed. The man probably never relaxed. He was most likely always tense.

No, tense wasn't the right word. He was always alert. As she surveyed him, she realized that alert was exactly the right word. And it was confirmed when he looked up, almost as if he sensed she was there.

"Good morning, Selena," he pushed away from the SUV and came towards her. "You didn't sleep well last night, did you?"

She laughed, shaking her head. "Not well," she fibbed. She hadn't slept at all!

"Change isn't easy. But you'll get through this. I'll help you."

Selena tilted her head slightly. "You say that as if it is a foregone conclusion that I'm taking the job."

He smiled confidently and took her hand, leading her towards the SUV. "You are," he announced. "So tell me what kept you up all night?"

She didn't dare reveal her nervousness about being close to him. And there was no way she'd admit that she was anxious about taking on so much responsibility. Instead, as she sat in the passenger seat of the SUV while he drove through the streets of Arlington, she talked about the moving process and driving across country, all the small things that had to happen before she could take on such an enormous challenge.

He took her to a hotel for breakfast and she discovered what a thirty dollar bowl of yogurt and berries was like. In her mind, the yogurt and berries tasted exactly like what she got in the grocery store for a few bucks, but what did she know? Maybe there was some secret ingredient, like unicorn glitter or something! She wasn't paying the bill, so she kept her mouth shut and sipped her green tea.

"How about if you fly out tomorrow with me and I'll show you around Denver, we'll go apartment shopping and get the ball rolling?"

She choked on her tea, peering at him over the rim of the china cup. "Tomorrow?"

He shrugged, leaning back in the plush chair. "You're taking the job, Selena. So, why wait?"

Frantically, she tried to think up reasons to delay. He was right, she *was* going to take the job. It would be stupid not to take the job. A promotion and a huge salary increase weren't something to turn down, especially since she didn't have strong ties to this area. She didn't have children that would be leaving their friends and schools. In the early hours of the morning, she'd come to the conclusion that there really was no valid reason not to take the job. Other than fear.

"Because I need to train someone to take my place."

"The HR department already has several candidates ready. Interviews are set up for next week with your boss."

She frowned, not liking the idea that she could be replaced so easily. But she pushed the thought aside. "Okay, well, I need to pack up my apartment."

"We'll be flying on a Rembrandt Cosmetics jet. Pack as much as you need for a couple of weeks and I'll hire a moving service to pack up the rest and ship them."

She held her breath as she stared across the table at the man. "You really don't hold back, do you?"

He smiled ever so slightly in satisfaction and her heart tripped over its feet. "Never. When I want something, I get it."

Selena could understand that philosophy. She'd wanted something, a new life, and she'd done everything within her power to make it happen. Now she had it and...why was she hesitating? After that horrible night so long ago, she'd vowed to embrace life and make herself...different. Stronger! This was simply the next step! She could do this job. He was offering her more money, more responsibility, a new life, and a new home.

With that thought in mind, excitement and determination to move forward obliterated her hesitation. "Okay. This weekend. I'll take the job."

His smile was slow, lighting up his eyes. She could barely

breathe as she watched his face transform. "I'm really glad to hear that, Selena."

Somehow, those words seemed personal. But surely he didn't have a hidden agenda. Looking down, she stared at the half eaten bowl of yogurt. She'd eaten all of the berries. Curling her fingers into fists, she had to fight the urge to pick up her spoon and shovel the rest of the food into her mouth.

Just nerves, she reminded herself. Face the fear and handle it. Don't let the past repeat itself, she told herself.

It was a mantra she'd had to incorporate into her life until it became second nature. But every once in a while, old habits reared their ugly head and she had to fight the old, familiar urges.

Chapter 3

Wow! Denver heat really *was* different! Amazing! The mornings were cool, crisp, and lovely. Selena pulled her sweater on, wondering if the air was cleaner here. If there isn't as much humidity in the air, wouldn't it be cleaner? Wouldn't the air particles move around more? She laughed as she lifted her face up to the morning sunshine. It certainly helped her move more easily! The heat and humidity of a Northern Virginia summer morning was oppressive. This air was invigorating!

She really liked it. Granted, this was her first morning here, but she liked feeling cool and dry instead of the muggy heat she'd left behind. Loved it, actually!

Even her run this morning had been amazing! Five miles hadn't ever been so easy and she felt rejuvenated, ready to tackle the world!

"You look chipper," a deep voice came from behind her on the sidewalk in front of her hotel.

Selena swung around, almost tripping on her feet. "Mr. Jones! What are you doing here?" she asked, more than a bit breathless. He was wearing dark jeans and a white shirt, open at the collar and untucked, but it was the kind of tailored shirt that narrowed at his waist, making him look...excellent!

Stop it! She'd had a stern talking to herself about lusting after one's boss. Nothing good could come of it.

"Nice shoes," he commented and she looked down at her sandals with the pretty beads decorating the straps. With a blush, she looked back up, shrugging dismissively. She absolutely loved shoes, probably had way too many of them but she wasn't going to change that part of herself. "They suit you." Was his voice softer? Possibly. Or it could just be her imagination. She'd been doing way too much of that lately. Imagining this man in all sorts of interesting positions. With her.

"What just went through your mind?" his deep voice asked as he stepped closer to her, his eyes narrowing as he took in her expression.

Selena groaned inwardly. "Um...just wondering where I should start looking for an apartment. I'm not sure where the best areas of Denver are for apartment shoppers." Wow, that was a whopper but nice save. She mentally patted herself on the back. Unfortunately, the look he was giving her told her that he might not completely believe her lie.

Smart man. She almost laughed at his disbelief, but then she'd have to explain her amusement and...well, better to just cut this off at the knees.

"What are you doing here?" she asked.

"I'm here to take you around to look at apartments," he explained. "I promised the service and I never fail to deliver," he teased.

She lifted her phone, feeling more than a bit awkward. "Oh! Um...I've got an app," she explained lamely. She'd downloaded an app that showed all of the apartments to rent as well as reviews and feedback about the surrounding areas and stores. "Thank you though. You probably have more important things to do on a Saturday morning."

He took the phone from her numb fingers, and began flipping through apartment listings. At that particular moment, she was intensely grateful that she'd done her internet searches on "getting over crushes" on her laptop instead of her phone. It had been late.

She'd been exhausted. Selena had a million excuses as to why this silly fascination with Reid Jones continued to flourish.

"This one is too far outside of the city," he told her and swiped left to banish it into Internet oblivion. "And this one isn't in a good neighborhood." Another left swipe.

This was helpful, she told herself, wanting to peer over his shoulder, but she didn't want to get too close. Even standing a foot away from him, she could smell the clean, fresh scent of him. All male and that pine scent that was...too enticing! Apartments, she admonished silently. She was going apartment shopping today, not Reid Jones shopping.

She lifted up on her toes, trying to see what he was doing. "Okay, well, what about those three? Are they in neighborhoods that might...?"

"We'll see," he interrupted, handing her the phone back. "Let's go take a look at them."

His hand on her elbow got her moving, but her mind definitely wasn't. She actually walked beside him for several steps before she realized what she was doing. Or not doing, which was walking gracefully. "Um...Mr. Jones..."

He swung around, stepping in front of her as he frowned down at her. "You're supposed to call me Reid."

Licking her dry lips, she tried to think. It wasn't easy. "Yes. Reid. Well, I don't..." She tried to step back but his hand shot out, stopping her. Her head whipped to the side and she realized that she'd almost stepped back into a family of four trying to hail a cab. "Sorry," she mumbled.

The family smiled and moved on, but Selena watched their teenage daughter glance wistfully at Reid. Selena empathized with the girl. It was hard to look away from him.

Shifting around, she moved so that she wasn't in the family's way, but she wasn't so close to Reid either. "Reid," she started again, but as she opened her mouth to say the words, he interrupted her again.

"Selena, if you think I'm going to dump you into a strange city and leave you to fend for yourself, think again. I'm not that kind of man," he said and took her elbow again, leading her over to a Jeep Wrangler.

"Of course," she muttered.

"What is 'of course'?" he asked as he pulled open the door for her.

She glanced up at him, then quickly pulled her eyes away before her mind started doing those silly fantasy-things again. "It seems like more than half the population of Denver drives either a Jeep or a Subaru. Everyone here seems to be super-sporty and outdoorsy."

He laughed softly and she tried to pretend that the sensual shiver wasn't hitting her. Again.

"Yeah, you'll get hiking fever before long. Tomorrow, I'll take you up into the Rockies so you can experience a *real* mountain."

She pulled back, frowning at him. "I've been hiking in the Appalachian Mountains, Reid."

He laughed, shaking his head. "That's not a real mountain." He leaned in slightly. "It's not a real mountain until you've got snow in July. Does the Appalachian Trail have snow?"

Snow? In July? Huh? "No but..."

He pulled back, shaking his head. "Not a real mountain," he announced and shut the door.

Selena burst out laughing, glad that he couldn't hear her since he was walking around the front of the Jeep. When he stepped into the driver's seat, she turned slightly. "I've heard of Grill-Envy and Car-Envy. But I never knew that there was really such a thing as Mountain-Envy."

He pressed the button to start the Jeep. "There's no 'envy' involved when we're talking about mountains. What you guys have on the East Coast is a series of hills. We've got mountains," he told her firmly, pointing a thumb at the western skyline. "That's a mountain!" he admonished.

Another chuckle as he pulled away from the curb, her eyes caught by the sight of his hands gripping the wheel. And forearms. Goodness, he was hot! There was a light sprinkling of hair on his forearms that enticed, teased. She wondered what his chest looked like. Was it covered with hair? Or was there just a light sprinkling? The hair on his forearms was light brown while the hair on his head was dark. She suspected that this man spent a lot of time in the sun and she sighed.

"What was that?" he asked as he pulled to a stop at a red light.

"Hmm?" she asked, trying to keep her eyes forward but it was hard. His jeans were soft and the muscles in his thighs pressed against the material.

"That was a big sigh. What were you thinking about?"

She cringed. "Um...just thinking about all of the apartments to see," she lied.

"Right," he replied, obviously not believing her.

"Turn right ahead," she directed, tapping her phone to find the directions to the first place.

"What's wrong with the hotel we put you up in?" he asked. "Why don't you just stay there for a while until you're more comfortable in the city?"

Besides the expense, she silently questioned? The hotel he'd dropped her off at several days ago was one of the most exclusive in the city. And he hadn't just put her in a room. Nope, she was living in a suite! It was huge and beautiful, with glorious views of the city in one direction and the mountains in another direction.

"My furniture arrives next week. The moving company your assistant arranged for me needs an address. I can't really tell them to just keep it in the truck until I find a place to live. I need to get settled."

"Agreed. I have a great idea, but let's check out these places first."

She wasn't sure she wanted to hear his "great idea", but she appreciated his help in getting her around town. Since she'd spent so much time at the office discussing the new marketing strategy with the various departments this week, she'd basically lived at the office, only coming back to the hotel to collapse into the ultra-soft bed at the end of each night.

Selena directed him with her phone's GPS to the first apartment complex and she smiled as he pulled into a parking spot.

"I don't like it," he announced.

She did a double take, looking at him, then at the nicely manicured landscaping, the well-maintained buildings with balconies for each apartment and even a community room and an exercise facility. "What's not to like?" she asked, looking around once again, trying to find flaws.

"It's just...not right," he said and put the Jeep into reverse, about to back up.

"Wait a minute," she yelped, putting a hand over his on the gear shift. For a long moment, they froze, both of them looking at her hand covering his. The tension spiraled and she curled her fingers away.

He spoke first to Selena's relief. She wasn't sure she could have spoken anyway. "The apartments are probably tiny and the kitchens not renovated. You need more than that."

She put her other hand on the door handle, trying to hide her reaction to that touch. It was hard, but she knew that she was silly to think about things like that. "There's nothing wrong with this apartment complex. I'm going in and looking around."

Selena stepped out of the Jeep, painfully aware of him

watching her. She knew that he wasn't *really* looking at her. Men like Reid Jones went for tall, leggy blonds or sultry brunette supermodels. Good grief, the man ran a multi-national cosmetics company! Gorgeous women surrounded the man. He was in charge of the marketing aspects of Rembrandt Cosmetics, which meant he supervised the selection of which models to use for their advertising campaigns.

So there was absolutely no reason he would be interested in a mousy woman like her. Yes, she worked hard to maintain her health by exercising and eating well. And yeah, she knew how to put on makeup. She was a trainer, after all. She knew all the tips and tricks, teaching the Rembrandt Cosmetics makeup artists on how to use a woman's features, highlight the best and hide the problem areas.

But to think that he might be interested in someone like her was just fooling herself. Remember George, she said silently as she made her way to the management office.

Stepping inside, she smiled at the receptionist who greeted her. "Hi, I'm interested in a one bedroom apartment." The receptionist smiled and opened her mouth to speak. But Reid stepped in behind her, warming her back with the heat radiating off of his chest.

"She needs a two bedroom at least. And nothing under fifteen hundred square feet."

"I'm sorry," the receptionist stammered. "But none of our apartments are that big."

Selena waved a dismissive hand. "I don't need anything that large. Just some place to..."

"Fifteen hundred," Reid stated firmly behind her. "Two bedrooms. Three if you have one."

Selena spun around, glaring up at him. "First of all, I can't afford fifteen hundred square feet," she told him firmly, poking him in the chest. "And secondly, you're being rude!"

He laughed, his hands resting on her hips. "You're going to need a place to entertain. Why wouldn't you..."

What? Entertain? As in dinner parties and things like that? "I don't entertain!" she huffed, pushing his hands away, but they came right back, even pulling her against him.

"You will. You're in management now. You're going to need the space. Entertaining and networking are part of your job. And besides," he pointed out with a wink down at her, "Denver is a more social place than Northern Virginia. People actually know their neighbors here. You need room to entertain, Selena."

She gritted her teeth, both to keep herself from shouting at him as well as to not moan at her need to press herself against him. Goodness, his hands felt wonderful! She could imagine pressing against him, feeling his taut abs against her stomach, letting his hand slide up her back and...

Shaking her head, she mentally banished the distracting images. "Reid, you're interrupting."

"There are resident areas in which you can entertain," the receptionist offered.

Twisting out of Reid's arms, Selena moved away and turned back to the woman. "Ignore him. He's not the one renting the apartment. I am and I only need a one bedroom."

The woman smiled, but it was a nervous effort. Obviously, she wasn't sure who to answer, but Selena smiled confidently as she nodded. "One bedroom, please. If I need to entertain," she glanced behind her, "then I'll figure that out when I get there."

She could have sworn he was growling. Maybe he was trying to say something and...she had no idea. The man was a mystery. Her gratitude for his assistance was disappearing now that he was doing that alpha male thing. Yeah, she liked it on a date or when she was interested in a guy. It was very rare to find a man who was confident and powerful, but didn't veer off into the self-centered, arrogant, irritating realm.

Right now, Reid was losing that battle.

The woman gathered up several brochures and spread them out.

"We'll just look at the apartments," Reid interrupted. "No need to give us brochures when we're already here."

His comment threw off the receptionist again, who was just trying to do her job. "Ignore him," advised Selena steadily.

The receptionist stood up, trying to appear confident, but she couldn't look Selena in the eye. "How about if we go look around and if you are interested, we can discuss the benefits of living here afterwards?"

One thing was good, Selena thought. This was the first woman she'd seen wearing heels. It was good to know that not everyone wore hiking boots or Birkenstocks. Which wasn't really fair, she thought as she followed the woman, ignoring Reid as he brought up the rear. The women she'd been working with at the office wore professional clothes. It was only her ill-informed perception of the people in Denver that had made her assume that everyone around here wore hiking boots. Looking back, she checked Reid's feet. Sure enough, he was wearing a nice pair of shoes. No hiking boots but from his disparaging remarks about the Appalachian Mountains, she suspected that he had at least one pair of hiking boots in his closet.

"Do you own hiking boots?" Selena asked the receptionist leading them into a ground floor apartment.

She looked back, startled. "Of course!" she grinned. "I have Monday and Tuesday off and I head up into the mountains just about every chance I get. It's gorgeous up there." She unlocked the door. "I take it you're not from around here?"

Selena's eyes narrowed. "I'm from the East Coast. We hike around the Appalachian Trails."

"Oh, those aren't mountains!" she laughed, waving away the possibility. "Wait until you get up into the upper elevations of the Rockies! The views are incredible! And discovering all of the different flora and fauna that somehow survive in those rugged areas? It's amazing!"

Selena kept her mouth shut, but she couldn't avoid a glance at Reid. Sure enough, his look said, "Told ya!"

She simply rolled her eyes and followed the woman into the apartment. It was a demo apartment, obviously set up by a decorator to show an ideal look.

"This is the best you've got?" Reid demanded, hands fisted on his hips as he looked around. "It's too small. Selena..."

"Don't say it!" she snapped, then was shocked that she'd spoken so firmly to the man. He was her boss, after all.

The woman hovered awkwardly by the doorway. "We have a fitness area, pool, and a fire pit where the residents gather on Friday nights for happy hour. Everyone brings their own drinks and gets to know one another."

"That sounds nice."

"Sounds cheesy."

Selena swung around, her mouth hanging open. "What's cheesy about people getting to know their neighbors?"

He moved closer. "First of all, you work hard all week. I've seen you over the past few days. You're exhausted every night. And secondly, Friday nights sound like a hookup time. I don't like it."

She thought about that for a moment and acknowledged that he might be right. Then again, he might be wrong. "I don't know. It sounds pretty nice. I come from an area where I never knew the person who lived across the hall from me. Never even saw them enter their apartment although I know someone lived there because there was occasionally music coming through the door. So, I think it might be nice to get to know my neighbors."

He moved closer, towering over her and his expression darkened. "You don't need to do it in a singles environment."

Selena agreed, but she was just being stubborn now. "And what if I *want* to meet single men?" she challenged him.

His eyes narrowed even more. "If you want to date someone then..." he stopped short, not finishing his sentence. Instead, he looked over at the receptionist. "She doesn't want the apartment," he announced, then took Selena's elbow, ushering her out of the apartment.

Reid was livid, so angry with Selena and the world that he felt like his head was going to explode. Opening the Jeep's passenger side door, he waited for her to get in. "You can't really *want* to meet a bunch of sleazy, single men."

She humphed a bit, but he relaxed when she slid onto the seat. "I might."

He couldn't stop the laugh, because he knew her well enough to know that she was just talking out of her ear now. "No, you don't. And if you want to date, I'll take you out."

With that, he closed the door and walked around the car.

He took a moment to wonder what the hell he'd just said. Selena was a goddess, no doubt about that, but she was sweet and nice. Completely unlike the women he normally dated. She was the kind of woman that a guy married. Not the kind that had relationships like what he normally had with women.

Hell, he couldn't even call his interactions with women "relationships". They were mutually satisfying liaisons that ended when he grew bored. Granted, most of the women he met and took out to the various social functions around town were a bit air headed. They looked nice, smelled nice, and knew the score. They were fully aware that whatever they did together would not end in anything that could be defined as a relationship and he preferred his affairs exactly that way.

So why was he getting all bent out of shape at the idea of Selena finding a guy that might give her what she most likely needed? She was a marriage and kids, two cats and a dog kind of woman. She wasn't the fool-around-with kind of female. She was hearts and roses. She'd probably expect her man to take her out for Valentine's Day dinners and snuggle on the couch watching a movie on the weekends.

The idea...well, it used to make his skin crawl but... he could imagine that with Selena. She was stunningly gorgeous with an incredible body. Definitely more toned than the other women of his acquaintance. From what he'd seen from the women he'd taken out to dinner, they starved themselves. Selena's legs...those muscles could only come from exercise, and hard exercise at that.

No, Selena definitely wasn't his type. But that didn't mean he wanted her to find some jerk who would have sex with her on a Friday night after happy hour and forget her name when he saw her poolside on Saturday.

How disgusting was that?!

"Where is the next place?" he asked, pulling out of the parking lot.

She folded her hands on her knees, drawing his attention to her hands. Delicate hands, he thought. Pretty nails. Not long and dagger-like, but neat and pretty. Hands he could easily imagine as they wrapped around...don't go there!

"I'm not telling you where the next place is, Reid."

"Good. We're done. You can stay at the hotel or–"

She laughed, interrupting his next suggestion. "I'm not staying at the hotel. And I'm not going apartment shopping with you anymore."

"Fine. That's settled."

She looked over at him and he could have sworn that her glance eased some of the tension he was feeling. He liked having her look at him. Was that weird? Yeah, probably kind of weird. He didn't care. She had beautiful blue eyes. The kind of eyes a butterfly might envy. He smiled slightly, thinking of Selena as a pretty, blue butterfly with stiletto heels.

"What's so funny?"

He shook his head. "Nothing. So you're done for the weekend. Good. Let's..."

"No. I'm not done. You're going to drive me back to the hotel. I'm going to get my rental car and go off to find an apartment alone. You're a liability." She turned those baby blues on him and he laughed.

Damn, she was cute when she wanted to be firm. "You're not going apartment shopping alone," he told her. "Where's the next one?"

She crossed her arms over her chest and shook her head. "No. Take me back to my hotel. I'm going on my own. You'll just mess up the next visit and I don't want that. I'm giving each of these places a fair shake and will choose one that works *for me*."

His smile broadened. No one ever challenged him when he gave an order. The fact that Selena thought she could...well, it was hot. And he kind of liked it. Not that he was going to let her get away with it, but he still liked that she wasn't intimidated by him.

"What's the next address?"

She pressed her lips together and he chuckled. "Okay, you think you're more stubborn than I am? Fine! We'll just head back to my place. We can go swimming this afternoon. It's going to be hot once the sun comes out and has burned off the evening chill."

37

Her mouth fell open as he put the Jeep in gear, ignoring her sound of disgust.

"Fine!" she grumbled and pulled out her phone. As soon as they pulled into the parking lot of the next apartment complex, he knew he wasn't going to like it. But instead of pointing out the flaws, he followed her into the rental office.

She told the sales person what she was looking for, still hanging onto the idea that she wanted only a one bedroom. He then followed them to the unit, enjoying the view of Selena's pert butt in the cute shorts and those long, sexy legs. He wondered what she would look like in shorts and heels instead of the flat sandals she was wearing. He could see her in heels that would make her shorts look even shorter. Yeah, he liked that image. Of course, if she'd worn heels, he never would have taken her to a place like this. Even now, some guy exiting the building couldn't help noticing Selena's legs. The idiot just about broke his neck twisting around to watch her, then almost ran into Reid. The bald guy stumbled backwards and Reid did nothing to help him as he adjusted his glasses.

"Keep your eyes to yourself," Reid grumbled, stepping around the man, following the two ladies into the empty apartment.

This one was just like the last one. A kitchen and den area barely large enough to fit a love seat and table with two chairs. The bedroom was so small, he doubted that a king sized bed would fit. And she was definitely going to need a king sized bed. He wasn't going to hold back, he realized as he watched her walk through the apartment. There was an obvious attraction between the two of them. It was powerful and she was beautiful.

Maybe he could change. For Selena, he could contemplate a relationship. Not marriage. Hell no, he wasn't doing marriage, but he'd love to see her when he walked into his house every night.

He knew that her smile would light up the night in a way nothing else ever could.

Yeah, this was going to be okay. A plan was slowly forming in his mind. A plan to get her into his house. No apartment would be good enough, or safe enough, for Selena. The guy ogling her a few minutes ago was a perfect example of what he needed to protect her from.

Looking at the muscles gently flexing in her arms, he suspected that the woman was perfectly capable of protecting herself, but still...what kind of gentleman leaves a woman to protect herself?

Not a good one, he told himself.

"I'm not even going to ask," Selena said as she led him out of the apartment and back to the car, her hands clenching the brochures.

He laughed softly, still thinking about his plan. Opening the car, he took pleasure in watching her long legs flex as she stepped into his Jeep. "Why aren't you going to ask?"

She slipped into the passenger seat. "Because you'll just point out all of the bad things."

He stared at her for a long, hard moment. He hadn't noticed any bad things, other than the ass who had ogled her legs. Reid dismissed the fact that he'd also been looking at her legs. And her butt. And now that he thought about it, her breasts were pretty amazing too. Hell, every part of her was beautiful! Including her eyes. And her smile. Yeah, her lips were perfect!

Focusing back on the conversation, he put the Jeep in gear. "And you want to put your head in the sand and pretend as if the bad things aren't there?"

She grinned up at him, feeling cheeky and confident. "Yep!"

He glared at her. "So the fact that you'd have a tiny washer and dryer instead of a full sized one doesn't bother you?"

He watched, almost laughing when her smile dimmed slightly. "I'll just do laundry more often."

"The sales person said that the only available apartments are on the second and third floors. And there's no elevator, so you'll be hauling your groceries up three flights of stairs." He paused, watching her enthusiasm dim further. "That's a problem during the months with good weather. But we get snow here in Denver. Imagine hauling your groceries along those pathways when they're covered with snow." The management company most likely cleared the snow with a plow, but he wasn't telling her that.

He could see her thinking about it. "Groceries get heavy when you're hauling them up that many stairs."

She huffed, blowing a wisp of hair off of her forehead. "Next place."

With a spurt of victory that he hid from her, he nodded his head with approval. "Where to now?" he asked as he backed up again.

Selena looked down at her phone. "The next place is in Thornton."

"No. Too far from the city. You'll spend too much time in traffic on Highway Twenty-Five."

She looked over at him as if he'd gone crazy.

"What?" he asked as he turned left instead of right to head back into the city. No way was he letting her live all the way out in Thornton. Nice place, but too far from him.

"You remember where I used to live just a week ago, right?"

"Okay, so Washington, D.C. has the worst traffic in the country, but you also lived in Arlington, which is very close to the city. You didn't get the full brunt of living outside of where everything was happening."

"True, the people who live in the outer suburbs had it worse. But you have to understand. People who live in Las Vegas learn to deal with the heat. People in Alaska figure out how to handle snow and cold. People in Florida...well, I'm not sure any of them really learn to deal with alligators or the pythons but...my point is, the traffic here in Denver is nothing compared to what people in DC have to go through every day."

He conceded that she had a point, but that didn't mean he was giving in. "You're going to need a place closer to the heart of Denver, Selena. You can't live in Thornton or further out."

"Why?"

"Because I said so."

Her laughter should have irritated him. So, why did the sound make him smile? Even Reid had to acknowledge that it really had been a lame response. In this case though, he didn't give a damn. "I'm the boss," he told her, thinking that was a better reason.

Another laugh and he vowed that he'd say stupid things all day long if only she'd keep laughing like that.

"All the more reason to live further outside of the city."

"What do you mean?"

She shrugged and shifted in the passenger seat. "Because I'm going to need to get away from you. I can imagine you being a real pain in the neck to work with. The further away, the better." She grinned back at him. "Besides, if I live further outside of Denver, I won't have to come into the city when it snows. I can simply stay home and revel in the..." her eyes widened when he laughed.

"What?"

He glanced at her as he maneuvered around several cars that were turning onto Speer Boulevard. "When it snows in Washington, D.C., the city shuts down."

Well, duh! Where was he going with this? It snowed in Denver. She'd seen pictures! "Right. Even the federal government shuts down sometimes."

He shook his head, chuckling a bit more. "That city shuts down if there's even the threat of snow." He looked over at her, a smug smile on his handsome features. "Here in Denver, we sweep it away and keep on going."

She shifted in her seat and he glanced at her. The smile on her pretty lips made him ache to kiss her, to feel her soft lips under his.

"Or get out the skis, right?"

He laughed outright at that. "Exactly."

He noticed her head tilt slightly. "I suppose I should get a different car."

He thought about the cute red roadster she'd been driving while living in Virginia. "That might be a good idea." Reid thought she'd look perfect in a car just like this one. "We'll go shopping for cars tomorrow."

Her eyes widened, but he noticed she didn't turn him down. Not that he was giving her any chance to say no. "Also, I know of the perfect place for you to live. The rent is reasonable, two bedrooms with twenty-five hundred square feet, pool access, fitness area with state of the art equipment, closer to downtown than anything you've looked at so far, has a full washer and dryer, and free maid and dinner service."

Selena frowned at him, not sure he hadn't just lost it. "I already looked at the apartments closer to headquarters. They are well out of my price range."

His lips curled slightly but he didn't look at her. "The rent on this place is reasonable."

He turned onto Alameda and, a few blocks later, pulled into the driveway of a gorgeous, huge house. "What's this?" she asked, thinking it was an apartment complex that she hadn't seen before.

"Come with me," he parked under a portico. He stepped out of the car, then waited for her to come around. "How's this?" he asked a moment later. They'd walked around a beautiful pool with a pergola covering one end to give it a bit of shade.

"This is beautiful." She looked around, swiveling her head. "Where are the other residents?"

He took her hand and led her through a sliding glass door. "Here. Combined kitchen and living room area. There are two bedrooms through there. One is larger than the other, but both have private bathrooms and walk in closets. Washer and dryer are off the kitchen pantry area," he said, leading her through the kitchen to a closed door where a utility room had a modern washer and dryer complete with just about everything she could need.

Turning around, she took in the gorgeous furniture, the elaborate lighting and the gourmet kitchen. Something occurred to her and she looked directly at him. "Who lives here?" she demanded, suspiciously.

"No one lives here. It is yours if you want it. Put your furniture in storage and use this furniture, or move this out and move your own in. Up to you."

She peered around him at the huge house on the other side of the pool. "Okay then, who lives there?" she asked.

He shrugged. "No one important. Do you want the place or not? If you want it, you can move in here this afternoon. We'll get you checked out of the hotel and settled in. Then we can go look for storage for your furniture."

Selena knew a trick when it was coming at her at full speed. Not to mention, she'd gotten to know him a bit over the course of the afternoon. He was stubborn and intuitive, arrogant but with a sweet, protective side. And he was hiding something. Something important.

Turning, she face him full on, looking up into his eyes to try and determine what he was hiding. "Reid, who lives in that house behind the pool?"

He watched her for a long moment, not giving anything away. "Technically, *this* house is behind the pool."

She rolled her eyes, trying for patience. And trying not to laugh at his stubborn refusal to answer the question. "You're splitting hairs."

His hand moved up, a finger curling around one of her dark locks. "You really are beautiful, Selena."

She pulled away from him, not believing him for a moment. "I'm not beautiful in any way, Reid. And you're avoiding the question."

His eyes sharpened. "You're kidding, right?"

Selena's heart froze and everything inside of her tightened with dread. Memories of past dates, the tricks and the taunts, the hope crushed under the cruel heel of men who...had hurt her more than she'd ever admit out loud. "Don't do this, Reid. If you don't want to tell me who lives there, then we'll leave it at that. But don't play with me."

Pushing away from the column he moved closer to her. His voice softened and she struggled to resist the sincerity and concern in his eyes. "Selena, who told you that you aren't beautiful?"

She crossed her arms over her chest. This was not a conversation she was going to have with Reid. He was muscular and smart, funny and confident; everything she'd always wished she could be. He walked through life knowing that he could have and do anything. Reid Jones was one of "them" while she...wasn't. She'd been the girl left at home every homecoming. She'd been the girl that...well, prom night wasn't something she thought about. Ever! It was so cliché, but she didn't care. People joked about their prom nights, about the things that went wrong, laughing at a dress strap that broke, or how they'd imbibed too much. Or whatever. But they'd never experienced the crushing pain of...the pain of being humiliated.

Turning away from him, she stomped towards the front door. "Fine! I'm calling a cab. This conversation is over."

Selena moved away from him, ready to storm out of the

beautiful house and leave him to himself. She had a phone and cash. A cab could take her back to the hotel and she'd just...

She didn't make it two steps before his arm wrapped around her waist and pulled her right back in front of him. "What the hell, Selena! You don't really believe that, do you?"

She tried to pull away, but he wouldn't allow it. So instead, she stood there, trembling with fury.

"High school," he guessed.

Those two words pulled at the wounds inside her. Her chin went up, trying to hide the pain from her past. "What about high school?" she asked defensively.

"It wasn't a good time for you, was it?"

She shrugged dismissively. "I was always on the honor role. It wasn't so bad."

He gave her The Look. "You know what I'm asking."

"Reid, my past is gone. I love my life, but I'm not living here."

"Why not?"

"Because this is your house, isn't it?"

"No," he came back with a completely straight face.

She squinted suspiciously up at him, her eyes showing her disbelief.

He sighed and rubbed the back of his neck. "I live there," he admitted, pointing to the house on the other side of the pool. "But only my annoying younger brothers use this house. Or one of them. Brant has his own place now so only Mack, my youngest brother, uses it. It was supposed to be just a pool house but the previous owners made it into a guest house so now, whenever Mack comes into town, or my baby sister, they use the house." He shrugged. "But my sister married some guy far away and the house is too small for her, her husband and her...the others that travel with her," he explained mysteriously. "My other two brothers," he shrugged, "one of them stayed here until his house was built, but Brant now lives on the other side of Denver. You'll meet him later this week. He's the COO of the company and a financial genius. Also a pain in the ass, if you ask me," he grumbled. "My other brother is a sheriff that lives in a tiny town in the mountains where he can do whatever strikes his fancy. But I usually have to go to him if I want to see him. He says that the city is too crowded. But if he comes to town now, he stays either in the main house with me or with my brother." He moved closer, his strong hands holding onto her waist once again. "Which is probably a better idea. Why not..."

"Don't even go there!" she laughed, relieved that he was being honest with her now. "There's no way I'm moving into your house."

"Why not?" he teased, liking the idea more by the moment. If she lived with him, he might be able to understand her a bit more.

"Because I need my own place," she asserted. "And..."

"Fine. Then you'll move in here. It's your own place. It has locks, a separate key, and everything you could possibly need."

"No."

He laughed, enjoying her stubbornness. "I'm going to win on this, you know."

She rolled her eyes. "I'm not falling for your charm, Reid. You don't offer your guest house to all the new employees of Rembrandt Cosmetics. I'm not going to be the first. It will be a trend that you can't sustain."

He shrugged and moved closer. "I don't want to kiss all of the new employees of Rembrandt Cosmetics," he said, his voice becoming deeper. Huskier. His eyes dropped lower, looking at her lips.

She stepped back, her mind going blank as heat flared low in her belly. "You don't...! I can't...!"

He smiled slightly. "Not yet. But soon you will feel comfortable around me and we can explore this tension between us." He stepped back, giving her space to breathe. "In the meantime, let's go get your stuff from the hotel so that you can settle in. I'll have my assistant arrange for a storage unit for your furniture."

Chapter 4

The cool air drifted around her, but it no longer chilled her. The chilling effect had stopped about two miles ago. But she wasn't stopping. It felt too good to be out here, feeling the air and admiring the mountains in the distance. This was living, she thought, thrilled that she'd actually taken the leap to move out to Colorado.

Thankfully, Reid hadn't allowed her to wobble on making the decision. She smiled as she rounded another corner, the mountains hidden behind the buildings and the trees. No matter, she thought, pushing herself harder. Down a few steps and she was on the Cherry Creek path. The water was low at this time of the year, but it still moved beside the pathway. She loved jogging this trail, listening to the trickle of the water. It seemed that everything in Denver invigorated her lately! Including the man who lived on the other side of the pool.

Flashes of his eyes yesterday haunted her and she wanted to laugh. Reid wanted to kiss her. Was he kidding?

Selena had no idea and, at this point in the morning, she wasn't going to worry about it. Right now, she was going to revel in the flirtations of a handsome man, knowing that nothing could come of the flirtations. Reid was her boss and neither of them would dare to mess with that issue. It was too...wrong. A relationship with her boss would create too many problems. Too many complications.

But still...

It was nice to think about, even if she'd never dare to follow up.

Nor would Reid ever push her in any way. Instinctively, she knew that and respected him more for it.

"You're going to kill yourself with this pace," a deep voice came from behind her.

She stumbled but, thankfully, caught herself in time. "What are you doing out here?" she asked as Reid jogged up beside her.

"I run this trail three or four times a week. I like Cherry Creek, and at this time of the morning, there aren't too many runners out here." He pointed up ahead at a runner coming towards them and they both moved to the side, letting the other person pass them.

"So, do you need help moving your stuff into the guest house?" he asked.

Selena smiled, thinking he was persistent and charming. "Who says I'm moving into your guest house?"

He laughed and she wondered how he had the breath to do that while running.

"I do. And you know that it's a better place than you'll ever find. More space and better rent."

"I decided last night that I'll take you up on your offer to stay in your guest house, but only because I want to find a house to rent instead of living in an apartment. So this move will only be temporary." They rounded another corner and jogged up a flight of stairs. "You were right about wanting more space. Until you showed me your guest house, I'd never thought about living in an actual house. But I like the idea."

"Wait, could you repeat that first part?"

She laughed, rolling her eyes. "You were right," she repeated.

He laughed. "Words to live by, my dear."

She chuckled and they moved to the side again as another runner passed by them. "I'm sure you're right about a lot of things."

"That's smart of you to acknowledge," he replied, causing her to chuckle again. "So when will you move in?"

"I'll do it as soon as I can. The hotel you put me in is too expensive."

"Don't worry about the hotel expense. I'll just tell Brant that it's for strippers and he'll approve the cost."

Selena stumbled slighted, but recovered gracefully. "I'm sorry, what did you say?"

He winked at her. "Brant, my brother. He's *really* into strippers."

They continued jogging for several more minutes while she absorbed that information. "Are you talking about the serious, stern man in the sharp business suit with the office on the other side of the floor from you?"

"The one and the same. He's the boring one. I'm the charming one."

She laughed, shaking her head. She didn't have the breath to jog while laughing this hard. "Your brother is too serious for strippers."

"He has you fooled. Which is normal."

"Normal?"

"Yeah. He makes everyone believe that he has a stick up his ass, but don't let him even pass by a strip club. He'd be..."

She gave up trying to run completely, she was laughing too hard. Bending over to catch her breath, she waved a hand to stop whatever he might say next. "Stop," she gasped. "No more. Your brother is too serious to be interested in strippers. Besides, you'd never even bring up the subject of strippers in your brother's presence."

"Oh, you'd be surprised at what I'd do to annoy my brother," he told her as they started back up and continued their run, heading back to the hotel now. "We were obnoxious kids growing up. And don't forget, we had a baby sister who needed to be subjected to brotherly hell on a regular basis."

"I can't imagine what the two of you might have done to your sister. I shudder with horror at the possibilities." They turned a corner, heading back the way they had come.

"I have two brothers, so there were three of us giving her grief," he corrected. "I'm the brains, the talent, the intelligence, and good looks in the family. Brant, the COO, is the middle brother and Mack is the youngest, but still older than my sister, Giselle. Mack is the one who lives up in the mountains and thinks he can control the world."

She turned to look up at him. "And you *don't?*"

He winked at her again as they slowed a block away from the hotel. "Oh, I don't think I can control the world," he told her, his voice husky and soft as the cool morning air.

She peered up at him, hearing the unspoken end of his sentence. He didn't think he could control the world. He *knew* it. And she didn't doubt him, she thought. The fact that she'd agreed to move into his guest house instead of renting an apartment was proof of his influence.

"So when are you moving in?" he asked again, bringing them back around to the original topic.

Selena stretched her calves, leaning against the building as she pressed her heel into the sidewalk. "The moving company arrives with my stuff in a couple of days. If it is convenient, I'll move out of the hotel tonight after work and..."

"I'll pick you up and help you get settled," he finished for her. "I'll even make dinner."

She opened her mouth to argue but he stopped her with his next statement.

"By the way, I sort of have a cat."

Selena blinked, not sure she understood. "How does one 'sort of' have a cat?"

He shifted on his feet and looked up towards the building. "Well, he...or she...just showed up one day and just...stayed."

51

Selena watched, trying to figure out what he wasn't telling her. "I love animals. Especially cats. I'm not allergic, thankfully, but I appreciate the warning."

Did his shoulders relax somewhat? Was he worried she wouldn't like his pet? That seemed ridiculous. He was so confident, why would he worry about a cat?

"Thing is, the cat...he...uh..." he rubbed a hand over the back of his neck, shaking his head slightly. "He shows his appreciation in...uh...well, when he likes you, he gives you presents."

"Your cat leaves you presents in the form of dead rodents as an offering of love. Is that what you are awkwardly trying to tell me?" she asked, trying to stop the smile at the idea of this big, powerful man defending perfectly normal pet behavior.

"Yes. He brings me presents in the form of various...wildlife."

"That's very sweet of your cat. You must be a kind owner. Cats only do that when they feel the need to pay back what you've done for them or out of love."

He chuckled. "I don't do anything for the damn cat, Selena. Trust me, he fends for himself."

"You don't feed your cat?" she asked, ready to head to the store.

"Of course I feed him. But...I have no idea what I do to deserve all of the presents he brings me. I'm not saying I'm going to do anything differently, just wanted you to be warned." Before she could reply, he stepped back. "I have meetings out of the office today so I won't see you, but I'll pick you up here after work. Say six o'clock?" A moment later, he jogged off, heading towards his house, which was another few miles away.

Selena didn't have a chance to reply because he was off again. For a long moment, she just stood there, admiring his... um...technique. Yes, his technique. Definitely not his butt. Or his shoulders. Even though both were exceptionally fine! For a man who sits in an office for twelve or more hours a day, Reid Jones was...impressively muscular!

Chapter 5

Selena lugged her suitcase into the bedroom, still feeling guilty about living here, but admitting that the luxury was amazing! Only a few weeks, she promised herself. Reid would eventually get sick of her being around, but this reprieve would give her enough time to find something she liked. Something that was close in to the city, had good shopping nearby, and wasn't painfully small.

The man was *going* to take her rent money though! She was going to be firm about that. She'd give him a check and, if the man didn't cash it, she'd figure out how to get him the cash. She wasn't going to mooch! No way. Her pride simply wouldn't allow it.

Standing in the middle of the room, she looked around, wondering where she should put her clothes. She didn't really want to put them into the dresser. That felt too much like moving in. And since she wasn't *really* moving in, just staying here until she found her own apartment, the dresser just felt wrong.

Closet?

Walking down the hallway, she realized that the walls held hidden closet space. Lots of closet space! Opening up the wooden doors, she realized that there were even hangars inside. Padded hangars! Good grief! She was used to buying the plastic hangars one could get at Target...something like twenty for five dollars. These beauties were probably twenty dollars each!

She lifted the stack of dresses and suits that were hanging from the metal bar on the moving box. The suits were hung on plastic hangars that worked perfectly well. No need for luxurious, padded hangars, she thought with a huff as she hauled everything to the closet nearest to the bathroom. Back and forth, she pulled everything out of the wardrobe boxes. At her last apartment, her clothes filled the closet. Here, her clothes barely filled up half of one of the three closets on one side of the hallway!

Having never really been in a relationship per se, she hadn't actually thought about what it would be like to live with a man. The idea of having a man dressing right next to her...and if that man were someone...oh, who looked like Reid...yeah, that would be amazing! And fun! She could just picture him coming out of the shower, a towel wrapped around his lean waist...or no towel would be even better...pulling on those dress slacks and a tailored shirt. Such a shame, covering up those shoulders!

Selena giggled, walking back to another box, picturing Reid walking into a meeting with nothing on. Nothing to spoil the view of his amazing body as he conducted the meeting.

"Nothing would get done," she said out loud, taking an armful of sweaters and...what to do with sweaters? At home, she stored them in a drawer. Eyeing the dresser, she wondered...perhaps it wouldn't be too bad to put them there. Just for now. She needed them at night, but the days were too hot for them. Looking down at her sweaters, she realized that she might need to get different kinds of sweaters. These were pullovers in wool and...one or two in cashmere she'd found at a deep discount last spring. She hadn't worn those because it was still summer, but once it was cold, she was pulling those babies on!

Jeans, leggings, summer shirts...all went into the various drawers and she was starting to feel a sense of accomplishment. Shutting the drawer, she turned around and...panicked!

"What are you doing?" she demanded, watching with horror as Reid peered down into the last clothing box. It was her underwear and...well, she really didn't want him to see what she wore underneath her suits. She worked out hard, and had a lot of sports bras. But even the underwear she wore to work or just hanging out, relaxing wasn't very pretty. It was...utilitarian. That was about all she could say about her tan, white, or black bras. She bought her underwear at Target, avoiding the pretty items, buying the un-fancy, unsexy, un-anything pieces that were comfortable and easy.

Reid gestured to the white, cotton panties in his hand. "Why do you wear things like *this*?" he asked a hint of horror to his tone.

"What are you doing in here?" she demanded.

"The front door was open. I came by to see if you wanted to come out to brunch with me." He peeked into the box again. "And you're not answering my question, Selena. Why?"

Her spine stiffened defensively, grabbing the underwear. "My underwear choices are none of your concern, Reid." She turned back to the box. "You shouldn't even know what kind of underwear I'm wearing."

"Why not? I'm going to find out pretty soon anyway."

She looked up at him, shocked by his assertion. "No! You're not!"

He chuckled. "Let's deal with the most important question first."

"Which is?" she demanded, closing the flaps on the cardboard box and shoving it under the bed.

"Why you wear such boring underwear."

She shrugged, unable to look him in the eye. "Because there's no need for anything fancier. Why waste money on something I wouldn't wear?"

His eyes widened. "You have no desire to wear pretty lingerie?"

"Absolutely not! Why would I?" She glared up at him. "It isn't as if anyone wants to see me in them."

She shifted uncomfortably under his direct gaze, afraid she'd just admitted something horrible to him. Something too revealing.

"So someone *has* seen you in your underwear," he murmured. He understood immediately. "And he didn't like what he saw."

She turned away, picking up a perfectly folded towel and re-folding it. "It doesn't matter. Not relevant."

Selena moved away to the bathroom, but when she came back out, towel – a.k.a. "shield" – gone and she wasn't sure what to do with her hands.

He was sitting on her bed, his elbows propped against his knees as he waited for her. "What happened?"

She shrugged. "As I said, not relevant, Reid. Did you need something?"

He stared at her. Need? Yeah, this gentle, strong, amazing woman was becoming a need. But more than that, he sensed a deep hurt in her. The more he got to know her, the more he realized that she was deeply wounded. Still strong and confident in business. But personally, she was shy and...wounded. There was no other word for it. His instincts told him that she had been hurt in the past. He suspected that someone in the past had not just rejected her, but had humiliated her.

How could someone do something so brutal to a woman who obviously was smart, brilliant even, and vibrant, funny, easy to work with, and a joy to be around...was beyond his comprehension. She was beautiful, strong both physically and mentally, and fun to talk with. Not to mention, she had a knockout figure and eyes that glowed with a humor born of intelligence, even if she might be scared to embrace some of life's greatest joys.

So why was she so afraid of him?

Because she'd been hurt in the past. The knowledge came with a fury unlike anything he'd ever known before. Yes, someone had hurt her, humiliated her and he wanted to find the man and pulverize him. Only a coward, a man afraid of himself would hurt a woman. And this wound wasn't the kind that showed on the outside.

Cat walked through the open door, rubbing up against his leg. Automatically, he reached down to pet the little guy, but he never took his eyes off Selena as she nervously stuffed clothes and towels away into drawers in such a haphazard manner, he knew she'd have to re-do it later.

He also suspected that the wounds hadn't healed on the inside. She'd just covered them up and pretended they weren't there.

"Yes. I came over to ask if you wanted to get something to eat. I noticed that you went for a run this morning, but you haven't gotten any groceries yet."

She stopped, painfully aware of the tug of happiness that hit her with his invitation. "Um...I don't..."

He gave Cat another rub, then stood up. "Come on. I think there are a few things we need to discuss."

He didn't wait for her to say no, simply took her hand and pulled her out of the bedroom. "Don't worry about unpacking. I'll help you when we get back."

He stopped by the kitchen, still holding her hand as he peered in her fridge, confirming that it was empty. "As I suspected." Armed with that knowledge, he led her gently out of the house.

She trotted after him, thrilled to be with him again, but also telling herself that she was getting in too deep with Reid. She liked his company and this sexual attraction wasn't going away. In fact, the more she got to know him, the stronger her feelings for him became.

But why did he peek in her fridge like that? "What did you suspect?"

"That you didn't have any real food in there." Turning to face her, he squeezed her fingers gently. "I'm guessing that your eating, exercise, and underwear issues are all tied up together, aren't they?" At her startled expression, he squeezed her fingers again. "It's okay," he told her softly. "I won't pry." His eyes moved over her features and Selena tried to hide her emotions. She was getting choked up about his gentleness and that wasn't a good thing.

"Please don't," she begged him, knowing that he wasn't just tenacious, but also perceptive. Too perceptive! She didn't want him to know about her past. She needed those things to stay there, hidden and unacknowledged. She'd dealt with the pain and moved on, grew stronger. She'd survived and thrived. And she didn't want him to ever know about that humiliating time in her life!

He sighed, that rough thumb rubbing over the back of her hand and sending shivers down her spine. "I can't seem to stop. There's just something about you, Selena."

Oh, she'd heard those words before!

Angrily pulling away from him, she moved to the other side of the driveway. "Yes, well, you're a nice man, Reid, but..."

She stopped, surprised by the peal of deep laughter.

"What?" she demanded.

"You know that being called 'nice' is the kiss of death for a man. Is that a trick you've learned over the years?" He shook his head as he grabbed her purse, handing it to her as he led her down the driveway. "It's effective, but it isn't going to work on me." He leaned down, closer to her and she held her breath, wondering if he was going to kiss her. Instead, he simply smiled and said, "I'm more stubborn than the other men you've met in the past. So you've been warned!"

Selena couldn't stifle the surprised laughter. Of all the things he might have said; more handsome, more charming, smarter, or anything else. Yeah, all of those applied to Reid Jones. But he'd gone with stubborn.

Why did that comfort her so much?

She was an idiot, that's why, she told herself as she followed along behind him. She felt a bit like a duckling being led by her mother, but in no way could Reid Jones be mistaken for a mother duck. Or anything feminine! He was about as rawly masculine as they came.

Speaking of which... "Why aren't you out shooting down a river on a kayak or climbing a cliff today?" she asked. "Isn't that what people in Colorado do on the weekends?"

He chuckled as he held open the door to a sleek, black sedan. "I've been known to haul out the kayak on the weekends or do a bit of rock climbing. I think we should start with hiking though. I was going to take you up into the mountains today, but we'll start with a relaxing day. Next weekend, you're heading up to the Rockies with me."

He closed the door before she could protest, and again, she had to laugh. The man definitely liked getting in the last word. Not that she was going to argue with him. She really did want to head up into the mountains and find out what all the fuss was about.

Looking around, she realized that this wasn't his Jeep Wrangler. The leather seats on this beauty were buttery soft and amazingly comfortable. She didn't recognize the logo on the steering wheel.

"What kind car is this?"

"It's a Tesla. All electric. I prefer to drive this around town, but it wouldn't work too well going off road when I get up into the mountains."

With a press of the button...nothing happened. No sound at all. But the dashboard lit up like a Christmas tree!

"It's beautiful," she sighed, thinking that this vehicle suited him perfectly. It was sleek, powerful-looking, subtly luxurious but without the pretentiousness of some of the more expensive models. "No Ferrari for you?"

He shook his head. "Nope. They are great to drive on the open highways, but I prefer a more environmentally friendly approach for driving around town."

He took her deeper into the city and parked near...the train station?

"We're having lunch at a train station?" she asked, surprised.

"I noticed that you prefer healthier foods and there's a great place in here that serves excellent food that isn't filled with grease and cheese. You'll love it."

A warm happiness bubbled up inside of her chest. The last guy she'd dated had become irritated with her when she'd ordered a salad at his favorite pub. He wanted her to have a burger with him, as well as some fries and a beer. Years ago, she would have loved that kind of a meal. She'd have smothered the fries in malt vinegar, added a bit more salt and dunked every wonderfully greasy strip of fried potato into a mound of ketchup. Probably even ordered a second slice of cheese for the burger, just to make it extra delicious.

Now, the idea of all that grease and salt made her stomach ache. She indulged in a burger occasionally, and even enjoyed the meal. But that was only an indulgence. After discovering exercise and eating cleaner foods, her life had truly transformed.

That made dating a bit more difficult though. Men might ask her out, but then argued with her about her food choices. When that happened, she stopped going out with them. She wasn't going back to that old life. Not for anyone!

When she picked up the menu, she was excited by some of the options. Most were even vegan, with loads of vegetables served up in creative ways. "Oh, this looks amazing!" she gushed, eager to try so many of the items on the menu, it was hard to narrow it down.

"What are you going to have?" he asked her, not even looking at the menu.

Tilting her head, she beamed across the table at him. "I have no idea what a squash blossom is, but I'm going to try the pepito salad and find out what a squash blossom tastes like."

He laughed as well. "A squash blossom is exactly that. It's the flower that forms on the plant right before the squash or zucchini starts to form."

They put in their order, he ordered the swordfish, and Reid was enchanted. "You're going to love that salad."

"You've had it before?"

"I've had just about everything on the menu at one point or another. This is one of my favorite restaurants because they change things up so often. They also find different ways to serve foods that we eat all the time, so it's creative. Plus, the restaurant gets almost everything from locally sourced farms."

"That's nice. I love restaurants that support the local economy."

He nodded in agreement. "So tell me what else you need to unpack."

They discussed the details of moving and Selena joked about the chaos and what it does to the mind.

When they finished their meal, he tossed money onto the table and took her hand. "Now for your next adventure," he said and Selena tensed up with the mysterious comment.

"I thought we'd head home and I'd finish unpacking so I can be ready for work tomorrow," she told him.

He shook his head. "No. You're not doing that. At least, not yet. You're coming with me and I'm going to explain a few facts of life to you."

Selena didn't like the sound of that. Not one little bit! "Uh... Reid, I'm pretty familiar with the facts of life."

He shook his head as he held the door for her. "No. You're confused about a few things." He led her down the street. "I remember sitting next to a couple in a restaurant a while ago. The woman was scoffing at an advertisement for a new kind of bra. It was an ugly contraption, made of some new kind of material that was supposed to be incredibly comfortable and with all of the bells and whistles that a bra might need...if you were a one hundred year old woman."

"Reid," she was silenced by his finger on her lips.

"No. Since you won't tell me what happened in your past to make you shy away from everything sexual, I'm going to explain things to you my way." He paused, chuckling when she simply rolled her eyes. "Good. Now, as I was explaining, this bra was incredibly ugly. The woman mentioned how ugly the bra was and that it didn't matter how perfectly the bra fit. If the bra is ugly, the woman wouldn't want to take off her clothes."

He watched as understanding brightened her beautiful eyes. Obviously, Selena silently agreed with the woman. "She's right. If a woman isn't wearing something that makes her look sexy, she won't feel sexy."

He could tell that she didn't believe him. "Think of it this way," he changed tactics, "when you go to work, you wear professional outfits. You put on your sexy heels and your pretty jewelry. You do up your hair, which, by the way, I love when you put it up." He grinned, winking at her. "Makes your neck look all hot and sexy. Gives me ideas about what I want to do to your neck." He chuckled when the expected blush appeared. "Anyway, the guy replied that she was missing the whole point of the bra."

Reid watched and waited, but the blank look in her eyes told him that she didn't understand what he was trying to tell her. "If the woman didn't feel sexy, because she was wearing an ugly bra, she's not going to want to take off her clothes."

The slight eye roll caused him to chuckle. "Yeah, I get that."

He smiled slightly. "Not only do you get that side of what I'm trying to tell you, but I suspect that you use your underwear as a defensive mechanism."

There was a long pause as she absorbed his words. They hurt. He was wrong! She didn't...she wouldn't....!

"I don't!" she snapped, wanting to argue with him that her underclothes were simply that – something to wear underneath her dresses and suits.

"You do. If your bras and panties are ugly enough, you are in no danger of taking anything off and showing me what's underneath." He waited...and it took less time. Damn, he loved her soft, pink blushes.

Belligerently, she held to her story, crossing her arms over her chest. "I don't understand what you're trying to tell me."

He took both of her hands in his. "Selena, the man in this story never grasped that pretty lingerie isn't necessarily for the man. His point was that the bra would be on the floor of the bedroom as soon as things started to get going and that's the way men like things." He laughed when she rolled her eyes again. "Lingerie is more for the woman. It's to make her feel good. A woman can wear the prettiest dress, but it's really what's underneath that makes the difference. It's all psychological."

She didn't want to believe him. "It's practical."

"And you're hiding behind that." He turned, walking down the sidewalk again, taking her hand and leading her along. "So here's my challenge for you. I'm daring you to wear something more interesting during the next few days. I want you to wear lingerie that makes you feel pretty. It doesn't have to be anything risqué," he added when she opened her mouth to argue. "Just something comfortable and pretty."

She looked up at the name of the store he'd stopped in front of, her eyes widening with horror. "I'm not going in there."

He rubbed his thumb over the pulse beating at her wrist. "Let me do this for you, Selena. Let me show you."

She looked over his shoulder one more time, the pretty lingerie in the windows grabbing her attention.

Her hesitation was all he needed. "Come on," he urged, leading her into the store.

"Nothing crazy," she whispered to him, moving closer as she looked around at all of the lace and silk.

"Nothing crazy. Just something pretty." Immediately, a salesperson walked up to them and smiled.

"How can I help you today?" she asked.

Selena liked this woman. She wasn't making eyes at Reid, pretending she wasn't here. She was older without a ton of makeup on, and she wasn't painfully thin, making her feel fat by comparison. Flashbacks hit her, the memories sharp and painful. It took every ounce of her willpower not to turn and run out of the store.

But Reid had challenged her and she wasn't one to back down from a challenge.

She decided right then and there that she would simply pay for every item that Reid thought would work and then return it later. She'd just make sure that none of the tags were damaged in any way.

Reid took the salesperson to the side and explained in hushed tones what he wanted. Then he handed her a credit card. The woman nodded, taking the payment and both of them turned to face her.

"I'm leaving," he announced. "This is Grace and she's going to help you." He took her hands and looked into her eyes. "She'll guide you through this. Don't worry. I'll be outside and I won't know anything that you've bought. Okay?"

Selena's muscles were so tense, she thought that she might shatter.

"Got it," she lied, her chin lifting ever so slightly. She wasn't playing his game, she thought resentfully. He could tell her that this was all for her benefit as much as he wanted, but she knew the truth. She knew what a guy wanted…

He squeezed her hands slightly. "I'm going to get a cup of coffee. Take your time and I'll be across the street when you're finished."

With that, he left, leaving here in the store to fend for herself.

Well, he could go to hell! She wasn't playing his games! Not this time! Years ago, she'd been stupid and gullible! She was smarter and savvier now. She could…

"I know what you're thinking," the salesperson said, interrupting Selena's mental tirade.

She turned to face the woman, thinking she looked kind enough. "I doubt it."

Grace laughed. "I bet I do. I've been there myself. Which is one of the reasons I opened this shop."

That got her attention. "What do you mean?"

Grace moved over to one of the walls and lifted up a beautiful lace and satin bra. It wasn't indecent and the cups looked to be covered with a soft material. Nothing was see-through, but the lace would lay against her skin, softening the edges. Even the color, a delicate soft, off-white, wasn't what she expected. "Why not try this on and let me know what you think?" She smiled when Selena opened her mouth. "You don't have to buy anything. Nothing at all. I can even give you a bag filled with tissue paper to walk out of here with if you don't find anything that you like. That way, your man won't know." Her grin widened. "It will be our secret."

Selena's tension lessened slightly, but she felt a thrill that the woman thought that she and Reid…! Another time, she told herself. Lifting her chin, she forced her lips to smile politely as she said, "I don't need to trick him. If I don't find anything I like, then I won't buy anything."

Was that admiration in Grace's eyes? "Good for you!" she laughed. "I love an assertive woman." She turned to pick up a matching pair of panties and bra set. "But just to prove him wrong, why not try this on? It would be better to have evidence that he's wrong. A man like that might consider it a challenge and," she peered through the doorway and Selena turned as well. They saw Reid coming out of the coffee shop, two cups in his hands and a newspaper tucked under his arm. "Well, it's always better to be well armed, don't you think?"

Selena nodded in agreement. "You make a good point," she replied. With a sigh, she took the items. "Fine. I'll try these on. But he's not buying me anything and I really don't think this is going to prove him right."

Grace's smile never faltered. "I'll show you to a dressing room. If these aren't torture devices, if they feel comfortable and make you feel pretty, then I have some other items that you might like as well. I'll bring them to you."

Selena walked into the beautifully appointed dressing room and eyed the pieces. They really were lovely. Holding them up to her figure, she couldn't help but wonder what they might look like on her.

Was Reid crazy? Or could these pieces actually do something to help her self-esteem? She ate well, exercised, and tried to live with confidence and kindness. Instead of rebelling against the idea of pretty lingerie, why not explore the possibilities? If small pieces of lace could increase her confidence, why wouldn't she try them?

In the end, her curiosity was too powerful to ignore. She pulled off her tee-shirt and shorts, stripped off her ugly cotton bra and panties and pulled on the lace pieces.

Selena was shocked...literally stunned by how comfortable the bra was. And the panty...well, it didn't quite cover her entire bottom, but...wow! It made her butt look amazing! As she moved around, the panty didn't ride up as she might have expected. It was incredibly comfortable! And yes, it really did make her feel more confident.

"Here are some other pieces," Grace called, handing several more beautiful sets over the top of the door.

Selena took them with shaking fingers, not sure if she should concede so quickly. Then she realized what she was thinking and felt foolish. Why ignore something that worked simply out of stubbornness?

In the end, she chose seven sets that really did make her feel good. When she walked up to pay for all of them, Grace had some other items. "How about just one pair of thigh high stockings?" she suggested. "If you like these," she tucked them into the bag, "then come back and I'm going to get you into a garter belt and stockings. You'll love the feel of them under your clothes!"

Selena stared at the woman, more stunned than she'd ever been in her life. Well, except for that one horrible night. But that night... it was so far in the past and she wasn't that that person anymore. She was...different.

Stepping out into the late afternoon sunshine, she felt Reid's gaze settle on her. And even from across the street, she could feel the heat in that look. He knew.

Her fingers tightened on the bag and she took a deep breath before walking across the street. They said nothing to each other and she silently headed back to where he'd parked his car.

"Are you okay?" he asked as he held the passenger door open for her.

Selena glanced up at him, not sure how to answer. "Yes. I think so."

Chapter 6

Selena slipped the beautiful, black lace bra up her arms, securing the clasp, then adjusting the straps. Looking at herself in the mirror, she felt...different. Yesterday, after purchasing the lingerie, she'd felt her whole mindset change. But seeing herself now, she wasn't sure...her body felt different.

Her phone rang and she glanced at the clock. She was going to be late if she didn't hurry up. Grabbing the black sheath dress, she slid it on over the lingerie so that she couldn't change her mind. She had to do this. Not for Reid, but for herself.

She answered her phone, a bit breathless even as she slipped on a pair of black heels. No jewelry today since she had no idea what to expect from her co-workers. Better to be safe than sorry, she thought as she stuffed a few more items into her purse.

"Are you ready?" Reid asked through the phone.

Selena paused and looked around. "Ready for what?" she asked.

"Brant, my brother, is back from a business trip. I'm going to introduce you around to the team and a few others today, so I'm driving you to work. I'm waiting outside for you."

Selena hurried out of the bedroom and peered through the glass doors. Sure enough, he was standing there, looking amazing in dark slacks and jacket with an open neck white shirt. He looked like every woman's dream man; sophisticated, casual, and confident.

Every woman's dream man.

He turned and stopped her through the windows. "I'll be out

in a moment," she told him and ended the call. Grabbing her lunch out of the fridge, which she'd made last night – while thinking about him– and her bag. With everything already packed, she straightened her shoulders, took a deep breath and nodded to herself. "This is it," she whispered.

And she walked out into the early morning sunshine. The heat was already starting to build, but she still needed a sweater. Probably for just another hour, maybe less. But she was still impressed with the difference in atmospheres here.

"I love these cool mornings," she said as she slipped into the passenger seat.

Reid watched her closely, wondering what she had on underneath the dress. She looked spectacularly hot this morning. The sleek lines of her dress skimmed along her curves and those heels...! Damn, he liked a woman in high heels. He knew that was sexist, but there was just nothing better to make a woman's legs look good.

Well, maybe when this particular pair of legs were wrapped around his waist, they might look better. He'd have to determine that once he knew the difference and judge accordingly.

"Reid?"

He blinked, realizing that he was staring down at her legs. "Right," he replied and slammed the door closed. Damn, this was going to be harder than he thought.

Walking around to the driver's side, he hurried his steps, realizing that he'd be able to see her legs as he drove to the office.

Okay, so it might be safer to watch the road rather than her legs. But he wasn't completely sure he could do it.

When they arrived safely at the office, he escorted Selena into the building, showing her around. When he reached the executive floor, he greeted several people, but kept moving along the hallway.

"This is my office," he indicated a set of double doors at one end of the hallway. "Let me introduce you to my brother. He's at the other end. Feel free to interrupt us for anything. We have an open door policy."

She admired that and knew that it trickled down to every level of the company. Reid and Brant Jones ran a tight company, but their policies were well known. She'd read several Jones brothers interviews, trying to discover the secret of their success. So far, no one had truly figured it out. Now that she was here, Selena suspected that the success of Rembrandt Cosmetics was due to the forceful personalities of Reid and Brant Jones. At least one of the brothers certainly had a powerful confidence about him.

"Brant!" he called as he stepped into his brother's office.

A handsome man, spectacularly similar to Reid, swung around in a large, leather chair, phone to his ear. But as soon as he saw Reid, he told the person on the other end of the phone call that he'd have to call them back.

"I take it this is the brilliant mind behind our new marketing strategy?" Brant asked, stepping out from behind a massive desk that had to have been custom built for this office. It was a fabulous steel and glass piece of art that she couldn't help but admire.

"I'm Selena Bailey," she replied, extending her hand. "It's a pleasure to meet you, Mr. Jones." For some reason, this man, who looked so similar to his brother in both height and coloring, didn't intimidate her like Reid did. There was something forceful about both brothers, but Brant Jones was...different. Yes, the hard features were there. The aura of authority and command were definitely alive and flourishing. But he was different.

"Brant," he corrected. "It's great to finally meet you. It's a shame it took Reid this long to get you out here to start the ball rolling."

Selena blinked. It had been less than a week since she'd left her old job and apartment. How long did this man think it would take a person to move across the country?

Shaking off her confusion, she smiled politely. "Well, I'm here now. I was doing a few things last week, but this is the week that we truly start moving on the project."

"Excellent! Your ideas are the best I've seen in a long time. And you have great timing. We were talking with advertising agencies that were competing to come up with the next best thing. It's good to know that we have brilliant in-house talent!"

Selena's smile widened and she felt a heat spread through her. That might be because Reid put his hand to the small of her back. But she was going to attribute the sensation to being eager to tackle a new project. And that project wasn't going to be the dynamic brother who was touching her! Nope!

"I heard you found a place to live, right? No problems there?"

"I'm all settled for the moment," she replied.

"She's living in my guest house for now," Reid announced.

Selena's head swiveled around so she could glare up at Reid. But she suppressed the angry retort. Turning back to Brant, she added, "Only until I can find a house to rent."

Brant's eyes narrowed, but then he smiled, a look passing between brothers. "Yes. I've heard that there's a housing shortage in Denver recently. Lots of people moving to the area."

Selena shifted, feeling uncomfortable suddenly. "I'm sure it's because of the weather. It's gorgeous here!"

He laughed softly. "You don't mind the desert heat?"

She chuckled, shaking her head. "You haven't been in Washington, D.C. during July or August recently, have you?"

The man cringed. "No. Not recently. I doubt many people would willingly travel there during the summer months if they could avoid it."

"Well, there are the free museums. And lots of other free things to do. So it's not a bad tourist destination."

"If you can take the humidity," he came back.

She grinned. "I think the tourist agencies sucker people into believing it isn't so bad. But when visitors get there, they realize that they should have come during April for the Cherry Blossom Festival."

"True. The cherry blossoms are amazing, but the crowds!"

She nodded. "Granted. The tourists are pretty intense, but nothing can beat the gorgeous weather and the cherry blossoms really are spectacular."

"I was there about two years ago during..."

"Yeah, well," Reid grumbled, taking Selena's arm. "As much as this little chit chat is helpful, I think it would be best if I showed Selena around to her office, introduce her to her team and help her get started."

Brant glanced at his brother, his eyes narrowing oddly, then threw back his head and laughed. "So that's the way it is?"

Selena looked over at Reid, whose face looked like a thundercloud. "Yeah. That's the way it is. You got a problem with it?"

Brant shook his head, his laughter dying down to a chuckle. "Nope. I'm glad that's the way it is. Congrats."

Selena glanced between bothers, trying to interpret the conversation. "What's going on?" she asked, wary and suspicious.

"Nothing," Reid said. So she turned to Brant, lifting her eyebrows slightly in question.

He smiled and also shook his head. "Nothing at all. Welcome to the family," he shook her hand again.

Selena smiled, not sure what "family" she'd just joined, but she assumed he meant the corporate Rembrandt Cosmetics family. Anything else just was too crazy to contemplate.

"Thank you," she turned to Reid, wondering what was next on the agenda.

"This way to your office," he told her.

Just as they were turning to head out of Brant's office, a beautiful brunette with luscious curves and bouncing curls hustled in, flipping through papers as she went.

"Here are the revised numbers you wanted on the new marketing strategy." She walked in as if she owned the place, a dare to her stride and laughter on her full, wide lips. The woman screamed sexy while her eyes challenged all in the room. As soon as she looked up from the reports she dumped onto Brant's desk, her eyes widened, as did her smile.

"Finally!" she laughed, clapping her hands. The lovely Italian accent only made her more alluring and Selena felt pale and gangly in comparison. "You must be the new marketing genius!" she exclaimed and stepped forward, extending her hand. But the woman didn't wait for Selena to shake her hand. Instead, she took Selena's hand enthusiastically. "It's great to see a new face on this floor. One would think with the beautiful sunshine and the glorious mountains in the distance, that the people here would be more laid back." She turned and gave Brant a meaningful glance, then looked back at Selena. "Not the case," she said, her accent thickening with whatever was going through her mind. "Come get me when you're ready for lunch. I'll take you to a place that will make you cry!"

And then she was gone. Selena stood there for a long moment, wondering what had just happened. The woman was like a beautiful whirlwind!

"You get used to her," Brant growled, his voice indicating that he had not yet gotten used to the amazing woman.

Selena laughed softly, shaking her head. "I hope not."

"This way," Reid told her and, once again, he took her elbow, leading her out of his brother's office. But not before she caught a look that sparked between him and his brother. Since Selena didn't know the younger brother well enough yet, she couldn't interpret the look, but she guessed that their silent communication had something to do with the woman who had just departed the office.

Chapter 7

During the next hour, Reid introduced her to several of the marketing staff, including her boss, the marketing director, and the team of ten people that would help her implement her idea. Her office was located right next to the marketing directors and, after Reid left her, the work began.

Over the next week, she worked long, hard hours. The team brainstormed ideas and slowly developed a plan. Marketing wasn't just about coming up with an idea. It was an eye opening experience and all of her business and sales knowledge was tested as she worked with this group of people who had helped bring Rembrandt Cosmetics from a small start up to a massive, international brand.

Selena woke up earlier each day, needing to get in her morning run so that she felt balanced, but then hurried through her morning routine in order to arrive at work as early as possible. There was so much to do, so many details to work out. It wasn't just the basic concept that she and the team had to create. Marketing was so much more than that. Models needed to be chosen, slogans refined, art work developed, commercial scripts written, social media strategy developed, television commercials refined...there was so much more to the world than she'd realized.

For her part, Selena was just the genesis of the idea. The marketing team would be the ones to develop and work up the ideas. While Selena brainstormed with the marketing team, she was in charge of developing the new training techniques.

She worked harder than she'd ever worked in her life, spending hours with the marketing team, vendors who might support their efforts, and the accounting department to ensure that their ideas would be profitable.

Selena took a great deal of pride in her work, wanting to be the best. She'd worked the makeup counter for Rembrandt Cosmetics during college and had always achieved the best sales with repeat customers who'd ask for her specifically. After college, she'd been promoted to training assistant and then trainer. After another couple of years, she'd been promoted to training the trainers for the district. This was the next step and she wasn't going to fail!

She got to work early each morning and stayed late, trying to research solutions to problems and find ways to make every idea better, more effective. By the end of the day, she was exhausted but always thrilled with her efforts.

And every night, she fell into bed and dreamed...not of color palates or moisturizing slogans, but of Reid and wondering what he might think if he ever saw her in her new underwear. Or out of it! The nights were long and she hoped that her co-workers never discovered how erotic her dreams had become lately. Especially since all of her nights and dreams featured their illustrious, devilishly handsome boss.

Chapter 8

"You ready?"

Selena jumped, surprised to find Reid standing so close. Again.

He'd sent her a text yesterday telling her not to go into the office, they were going hiking. She hadn't seen him all week, too busy with the marketing plans. Usually, his car was still in the garage when she left in the morning and she got home later than he did.

And boy, she missed him! Hiking and Reid, what an enticing combination. She had no idea how to tackle a mountain. And she didn't think she had it in her to tackle Reid, but she loved the idea of trying both. A girl could dream, she told herself.

Today, he looked amazing in a pair of shorts and tee-shirt, the material stretching across his shoulders, straining along his arms where his muscles pulled at the material. He had on a hat, sturdy hiking boots and a pair of sunglasses hung from his neck. Goodness, he looked yummy!

She took a deep breath and stepped out of the guest house, tugging on the knob to make sure it was locked. Not that she needed to verify that it was locked. She just needed some reason to pull her eyes away from Reid's enticing shoulders.

She noticed that he was carrying a backpack. "What's in the bag?" she asked, sliding her driver's license and some cash into her back pocket.

"Is that what you're planning to wear?" he asked, taking in her tan shorts and blue tee shirt. She'd pulled on sneakers for the hike, knowing that it would be too rugged for a pair of sandals or flats.

Selena looked down at her outfit, then back up at Reid, confusion in her eyes. "Um...yeah?" she replied, thinking it should be pretty obvious that she was planning to wear the shorts and shirt. "Is there a problem?" She looked up at him warily. "You said this would be an easy hike, nothing crazy."

He laughed softly. "Oh, honey. You're cute." He bent down and kissed her, shocking her further. "Open the door. You're not ready."

Selena was still reeling from the kiss, wondering if it would be too revealing to lick her lips so she could taste him. Probably, she thought. But oh, the temptation.

Shaking her mind free, she blinked up at him. "What am I missing?"

He chuckled. "Hiking boots for one. But I'm guessing you don't have any, do you?"

"Uh..." she had about twenty pairs of heels in various colors, another four pairs of sandals, an old pair of running shoes and... well, her slippers. Because every woman needed a pair of soft slippers. They were old, broken in, and incredibly comfortable. As for boots, she had a black pair and a brown pair, a few pairs of ankle boots...nothing that he would consider appropriate for hiking.

Looking down at her footwear, she shrugged, confused. "What's wrong with my sneakers?"

"Nothing," he replied with a devilish look in his eyes, "if you're sneaking around. Or going grocery shopping. Otherwise, they're not going to work. Not in the higher elevations."

She huffed a bit, but she wasn't sure exactly why. "You told me that this would be an easy hike. What's going on, Reid?"

"Trust me, Selena. The Rockies are...well, rocky. You're going to need better protection for your feet and more support for your ankles. We'll be climbing over rocks and ducking under waterfalls." He held up a hand to stop her protest, "Yes, this is going to be a relatively easy climb and I guarantee that you're going to love it. You also need a wool sweater and a waterproof jacket. It might be July here in Denver, but up in the mountains, it's still cold. There might even be snow."

She pulled back, latching onto one word. "Climb?" she asked, her tone a bit strangled. "Did I mention I'm not a huge fan of heights?"

He took the key out of her hand and unlocked the door. "You're going to learn to trust me, Selena. And today, you're going to enjoy your first hike in the Rocky Mountains. I promise, I won't let you get hurt. But that starts with being prepared with proper clothing and footwear."

He stepped into the guest house, dumping his backpack on the floor by the door before moving through the house to the back, not even pausing before entering her bedroom.

"Reid, what are you doing?" she demanded, hurrying after him.

"You need a sweater. Where do you keep them?" he asked, opening drawers. He didn't stop until he found them. He lifted several of them up, rejecting each one. "No, cashmere won't work on today's hike." He turned to hold the soft material up against her. "But I will enjoy seeing you in this once the weather cools down. He leaned forward and kissed her again. "You'll look...pettable."

She blinked, but before she could respond – again – he'd already gone back to sifting through her sweaters. "Nope. None of these will work for today's hike. You'll just have to borrow one of mine. I have an extra in my car."

With that, he closed the drawer and turned to the wardrobes that were built into the wall heading to the bathrooms. "What are you doing?" she demanded, trying to rush ahead of him so she could block him. No way did she want him going through her shoes! She loved shoes! He'd make fun of her shoe collection!

Unfortunately, her rush to get ahead of him and block his invasion only gave him an easy way to torment her further. Leaning a hand on either side of her head, Reid looked down at her, a dark eyebrow raised in question. "Interesting reaction," he purred teasingly.

"I don't have hiking boots," she told him, trying to be firm, but he was just so darn close!

She wasn't taking the bait though. She could resist making a fool of herself. It didn't mean anything, the way he was leaning into her. It was just his way. She understood that now. Don't be a fool, she mentally chided.

Deciding to be straight-forward, she straightened to her full height. Poking him in the only spot she suspected might be soft, the point right under his collar bone. She was wrong. It was just as firm as the rest of him appeared. "Listen to me, Reid. And listen carefully. I'm not one of those silly women who fawn all over you just to give you a chuckle later on, okay?"

He stared at her but she continued.

"You keep leaning into me like this, and I'm sure it works on the other ladies, but I want you to stop. I know you're not interested in me. Not seriously. So let's stop the pretending."

"Are you...?"

"I'm not finished," she cut him off, holding up a hand to stop whatever it was he'd been about to say. When he closed his mouth, his eyes still confused, she continued. "I have a lot of shoes. I like shoes. No," she corrected, shaking her head. "I *love* shoes. And I have a lot of them. But none of them would be appropriate for hiking. Got it?"

Reid pulled back slightly. She'd just thrown a lot at him and he wasn't sure which to tackle first. He looked down at her, noting her closed off expression. It suddenly hit him why she'd been pulling back whenever he got close. She'd been deeply, cruelly hurt. By a guy pretending to be interested in her? It seemed impossible. But as he watched her, her vulnerability struck him. Hard!

He wanted to wrap his arms around her and tell her that whoever had done this to her was an ass. A complete and utter ass! Women should be treated with respect. Someone hadn't realized what a treasure Selena was and...she'd never fully recovered.

Okay. He understood that. Had suspected it during their previous conversations. But the shoe issue? Why in the world would she care about that?

"Selena, there are a lot of issues I'd like to discuss with you after that little tirade, but let me first assure you that I absolutely love your legs. I love the shoes you wear, so there's zero chance that I'm going to tease you about the number of shoes you own, simply because watching you walk is like watching art. Your walk is sensuous and your legs are gorgeous! Never doubt that, honey." He smiled slightly, tilting his head to the side as he observed the confusion and disbelief wash over her. "You don't believe me, do you?"

She shrugged, crossing her arms over her stomach. "In my experience, men are not the most trustworthy species."

He smiled slightly. "Okay, fair enough. Something in your past has given you a distrust of men. Interesting comment and we'll explore that." He saw the panic enter her eyes and chuckled. "But right now, we need to hit the road. So, since you don't have anything resembling hiking boots in there ..." he stepped back, pulled his cell phone from his pocket and dialed a number.

He watched her carefully until his friend answered the phone. "Hey, I need a favor. I have an emergency need for hiking boots. Can you help me out?" He listened to his friend, but didn't really hear the words. Reid was too fascinated with the emotions flitting over Selena's beautiful features. She was horrified that he was calling someone so early in the morning, which he thought was hilarious. Soon, she would understand that many people who loved to hike, preferred to be up early in the morning, getting out to the trails or branching out into the woods so they could find their own path. Either way was a great way to enjoy the peace of being in the mountains.

"Thanks," he said, still watching her. Ending the call, he winked at Selena. "We need to hurry," he took her hand. Pulling her out of the guest house, he led her outside to the Jeep, ignoring her sputtering confusion.

"Where are we going?"

He shook his head. "You're going to have to trust me. You don't yet," he said, stopping her response as she'd done earlier, "but through my slow, evil plan, I'm going to earn your trust."

He loved hearing her melodic laughter as he walked around to the driver's side.

When he stepped into the Jeep, she said, "I'm not sure an evil plan is the best way to gain a person's trust."

He shook his head as he put the Jeep in gear. "With you, honey, I'm guessing it might be the only way. But I'm willing to shift tactics if I suspect one way isn't working." He glanced over at her a moment before he turned right out of his driveway, heading towards the highway. "You're eventually going to trust me, Selena. It's just a matter of time."

"Why?"

He shrugged. "Because I'm a very trustworthy fellow," he replied, winking at her. In about an hour, they would be in full sunlight and he'd be able to see her properly. But for now, he was content to just be with her.

Selena laughed, then relaxed back against the leather seat. "You have your moments of charm," she admitted. "But trust? Don't hold your breath."

He got off the highway a moment later and headed towards a shopping mall. "Where are we going?"

"You need hiking boots."

"The stores aren't open yet. My sneakers will be fine," she assured him. "I'll take it easy."

He shook his head. "Nope. I'm making sure that your first time in the mountains won't result in a twisted ankle or blisters."

She wasn't sure she believed him, but that was pretty normal around Reid.

"Come on," he said and parked in the empty parking lot. As soon as they pulled in, another car drove up and a sleepy looking man stepped out of the vehicle. "Are you Reid Jones?" the man asked.

"Yep. Thanks for meeting us here," Reid said, shaking the man's hand.

"No problem. Getting a call from my boss sort of jump started my morning. Happy to help out." He eyed Selena's shoes. "Size seven?" he asked.

"Seven and a half," she replied, feeling shock and embarrassment as she realized what the solution for her footwear problem was. Reid had called the shoe store owner who had jumped out of bed before dawn to open the store so that she could get fitted for hiking boots. Great!

But ten minutes later, she had chosen a pair of hiking boots as Reid thanked the guy. She even had some special socks that would protect her feet from blisters.

As they walked out of the store, boots and socks in hand, she shook her head at his audacity. "That wasn't necessary."

"Sure it was. I want your first experience hiking in a real mountain to be good. Besides, the guy owed me a favor."

She cringed. "And you burned up that favor by asking his store manager to get to work five hours before he needed to?" She asked as they both stepped back into the Jeep.

"Yep!" he replied and swung the vehicle around in the parking lot. "Now, we need breakfast."

"I've already eaten," she told him, thinking of the oatmeal she'd consumed before he'd knocked on her door.

"Probably not enough," he replied, shaking his head. "You need a lot of calories. First of all, you'll be walking uphill for most of the morning. Also, it's cold, so your body burns more calories than you might think." She glanced at him warily and he laughed. "Trust me, Selena."

She shifted uncomfortably in her seat. "I won't ever trust you, Reid."

"And why is that?"

She crossed her arms over her chest. "Suffice to say, that I've learned the hard way that trust isn't something that I offer to men. At least, not on a personal level."

He smiled slightly, but she had no idea what might be going through his head. "What?"

Once again, he simply shook his head. "You'll learn."

She didn't have time to ask him more since he turned into a parking lot that seemed to be teeming with cars and people. "Come on. You're going to love breakfast," he assured her.

She stepped out of the Jeep, ready to just turn down the food. But as soon as she moved away from the vehicle, she was struck by the intense smell. Bacon...cheese...eggs...! It all smelled heavenly! She hadn't had bacon in...well, years! But at the first whiff, her stomach roared, telling her how hungry she already was even though she'd eaten oatmeal sweetened with strawberries about an hour ago.

Pulling back, she shook her head, refusing to step any closer to the diner where people were walking in and out, most of them carrying huge bags of what was most likely food.

"What's wrong, Selena?" he asked, realizing that she was definitely scared of something.

She shook her head and glared up at him. "I have to go," she told him urgently. "I can't be here."

He stopped, not pulling her further. "Honey, what's wrong? It's just food."

Pressing her lips together, she fought against the old urges. She looked at the bustling crowd of people. They all looked happy and delighted with their pre-hike meal. But they hadn't...they'd never...

Looking back up at him, she saw the patience in his eyes, the waiting until she felt she could tell him. "It isn't *just* food to me," she admitted, not knowing of any other way to explain it to him. But the expression in his eyes told her that he didn't understand. "Food is...well..."

He put a hand to her cheek, looking down into her blue eyes. "What? What happened Selena?"

She closed her eyes and stared up at him, shame hitting her hard. "I used to be anorexic, Reid," she whispered. It felt like a shameful admission. "I was hugely overweight in high school. Then in college, I..." she pressed her lips together, refusing to tell him of her ultimate humiliation. "Well, I have issues with food. Bacon is a trigger for me. It messes with my head."

She opened her eyes and looked up into his dark ones pleadingly. "Please. I need to not be here."

He stared at her for a long moment, then nodded. "That must have been difficult for you," he said, pulling her into his arms.

Selena stood there in the warmth of his embrace for a long moment, inhaling his clean, masculine scent and avoiding the almost-overwhelming desire to inhale the smell of bacon. It was hard, but she moved closer to him, using his scent to help her through the urges. Closing her eyes, she fought the need, and eventually won.

"I can't imagine what you went through. I can't understand, but I want to help." He pulled back, but didn't release her from his arms. "You still need more food. This is your first hike and I really want you to enjoy it but you need to eat," he squeezed her gently, stopping her from arguing with him again. "How about if you stay in the car and I'll run in and get something to eat?" He kissed her forehead soothingly. "Does an egg white only burrito with veggies and cheese sound okay?" he asked gently.

She thought about it for a long moment, trying not to smell the bacon. "Yes. Yes...fine. That would be fine."

"Okay, I'll be right back." He first held the Jeep's passenger door open for her, closing it firmly before he walked into the diner.

Selena watched him, feeling foolish for reacting so strongly to the smell of bacon. But there was just something about the strong smell, the comfort of the bacon and the fat and the rich flavors that threw her back into her old insecurities.

Five minutes later, he walked back out, a huge bag in his hand and he smiled, waving to others as he went.

She stared at him, at the long, strong legs that she could see with his shorts. The dark hair along his skin, lighter on his forearms and the rugged look of his jawline since he hadn't taken the time to shave this morning...it all added up to a virile, amazing male. An enticing, dangerous male that was starting to get to her.

"Here," he said, handing her a paper-wrapped...something.

"What is it?"

"Just what I promised. An egg-white burrito with extra veggies and cheese. You'll love it."

She unwrapped the paper and looked down at the burrito. "It looks like it was just made, but you were only in there for about five minutes. Maybe even less."

He smiled as he pulled his own out of the bag. Well, three of them, actually. "Yeah, that place is ingenious. The diner is a regular stopping point for hikers on the weekends. They make up huge batches of burritos of different kinds, put them all in a line and people just grab what they need, pay for them at the end of the line and head on out. They don't make anything other than burritos at this time of the morning."

She took a bite, shocked by the explosion of flavors. "Oh wow!" she breathed. "This is amazing!"

He nodded, taking a bite of his own. "Yeah, they use a lot of herbs in their eggs. That's what makes the difference. And in this area, there's a ready supply of organically grown vegetables as well as range raised chickens for eggs. You can taste the difference, right?"

She nodded, not bothering to say anything since her mouth was full. Swallowing, she wiped her mouth with a napkin. "Oh, this is great!"

He agreed, and they sat in the privacy of his Jeep while they ate. Looking around as she finished up her burrito, she noticed that almost every vehicle here was either a Jeep or a Subaru. "Lots of people heading to the mountains," she observed, thinking out loud.

"There are different waves of people that come through for meals at the diner. This is just the morning wave. There are others who prefer the sunsets and will start off a bit later in the morning or afternoon, depending on their overnight options."

"Overnight?" she asked, thinking it wouldn't be a good idea to be out in the mountains overnight. "Doesn't it get cold overnight?"

He laughed. "Honey, it's going to get cold this afternoon. We're climbing to the higher elevations. There might be a bit of snow."

She nodded her head. "I suppose that makes sense since, even from a distance, one can see the snowcapped mountains."

They finished their breakfast and she took the bag, tossing it into the trash as they drove out of the parking lot. "Okay, now you're going to fall in love with hiking," he promised.

Twenty minutes later, he pulled off of the road into a small parking lot. There was a trail that she could see disappearing into the woods and the sun was finally coming up over the mountains.

"We're going to take this slow and easy so that you don't get blisters from your new hiking boots, okay?"

She agreed, nodding as she tied the sweater that he'd handed her around her waist. It looked huge, but then again, anything that he lent her was going to be massive on her. The guy was about a foot taller than she was and had shoulders that seemed as if they could take on the world. Perfect shoulders, she thought with a quiet sigh.

He grabbed the heavy backpack, tossing it over his shoulders like it weighed nothing at all.

"Want me to carry that for a while?"

He grinned and shook his head. "Nah. I've got this."

"What's in it?" she asked, curious despite herself.

"Water bottles, protein bars. Another fleece pullover for each of us. Matches in case of an emergency, first aid kit, GPS and compass, two light rain coats, knife, and sunscreen."

Her eyes widened. "Wow! All of that?"

"You learn to be prepared. There isn't an easy escape route here in the Rockies. Even park rangers, who know these woods pretty well might have a hard time finding hikers if they get lost."

"Sounds fair, although, even with a GPS or compass, I'm not sure if I could find my way out of a bag."

He laughed. "Oh, I have so much to teach you," he replied. And for some reason, his words sounded naughtier than he intended them. Then again, looking up into his dark eyes, maybe he had meant them to be salacious.

Rolling her eyes, she accepted the bottle of water he handed her. "You're a bad man," she muttered.

"And you're going to enjoy every moment of my bad-ness," he promised.

She blushed, but turned away before he could see the pink staining her cheeks. She walked beside him as they entered the woods, amazed at the silence.

"It's so quiet," she whispered reverently.

"That's one of the things that I love about hiking," he replied. "The silence. The fact that I could literally get lost in these woods and never come out. It's a bit intimidating and thrilling at the same time."

As they hiked, he gave her interesting facts about the trees and bushes around them, what the native Americans used them for and why, how they used to hunt and what to do in case of an emergency.

"What do you think you should do if you are surprised by a bear?" he asked.

They were stepping up on rocks so she was ahead of him at that particular moment. She paused and looked over her shoulder. "Run faster than you?" she offered.

He threw back his head and laughed. "Okay, that's a good answer."

She finished climbing, putting her hiking boot exactly where he told her to. She was out of breath when they reached the top, and he handed her another bottle of water. "Here, drink slowly, but take as much as you can. It helps to avoid altitude sickness and helps your body function."

She took the bottle and perched on a rock, looking out. She'd just lifted the bottle to her lips when she realized where they were. "Wow!" she whispered, the water forgotten as she stared out at the view.

He turned around and smiled. "Yeah, pretty spectacular, huh?" he agreed, settling down next to her. For a long moment, they just stared out at the view, seeing the other mountain peaks off in the distance, and the plains further out. The trees were pretty amazing as well, the pine and aspen blanketed the hillsides up until the oxygen was too thin for trees to grow.

"It's called the timberline," he explained, following her gaze. "It's the altitude at which the trees can no longer grow. There's not enough oxygen, water, or heat for them to survive."

She nodded silently. Making noise seemed like a violation of the moment. So for a long time, they just sat there looking out at the view.

"Thank you for this," she murmured softly. "It's more amazing than I imagined."

He handed her a protein bar and they sat there in companionable silence, looking out at the views. The bars weren't the easiest to eat, but they were filled with calories and protein, not to mention, the bars didn't add a lot of weight to one's pack. And even though she'd had oatmeal and the egg burrito, Selena discovered that she was famished!

"Want to tell me about it?" he asked her.

Selena looked down at her feet. "Tell you about what?" she asked, but she knew exactly what he meant.

"About what happened earlier?"

She thought about it for a long moment, then decided that he deserved to hear the story. "When I was in college, my body image became distorted. I obsessed about losing weight, to the point that I couldn't think about anything else. My grades slipped and I was having trouble sleeping. It got to the point that I started skipping classes just so I could spend more time at the gym. Eventually, I spent all of the allowance my parents sent me on exercise classes and I just sort of...stopped eating."

"Completely?" he asked.

She shook her head. "No. Not completely," she laughed self-deprecatingly. "I was so heavy in high school and...well, I needed the control. Not eating was my way of controlling my world. So yes, I would eat, but not enough to sustain my body or repair the muscles I'd used while exercising." She stopped, thinking back to that miserable time. "I'm better now, but it took me a long time to figure out how to come back from that. Time and a great therapist." She looked at him carefully. "There are some foods that trigger memories. Bad memories. I'm so sorry for freaking out like that, but bacon is just one of those triggers. I avoid the smell, just because it brings back those memories."

"How long were you sick?"

She smiled, grateful to him for understanding that she was sick and not crazy. "Less than a year. My mother realized what was going on and forced me to get help." She stuffed the protein bar wrapper into her shorts pocket and stood up. "I have a much better body image now, thanks to that therapist, but it is a struggle." She took a deep breath. "As long as I don't smell bacon or a few other foods, everything is good."

He stood up as well, pocketing his own wrapper, but she could tell from the look in his eyes that he wanted more of the story. "Is that why you don't date?"

She stepped back, careful to not step too close to the edge of the trail because there wasn't much beyond that except for a steep drop. "I date."

"You won't date me."

Selena's heart raced with his words. Oh, if he only knew about the fantasies she'd woven with Reid as the star! Shaking her head, she sighed. "Because you're not serious."

"I'm not?" he asked in surprise.

She shook her head. "Nope.

"So, you will only date men who are serious about relationships?"

She stopped and looked up at him, a realization dawning. "Actually...no."

"Why not?"

"Because..." She wasn't exactly sure why. The thought struck her that she hadn't dated anyone in...a long time!

"Because...?" he prompted.

Selena stopped walking and looked back at him. "I don't know why."

He moved closer, not touching her. "Perhaps I can offer a reason to change your status?"

She wanted to back up, to put some space between them, but she couldn't move. Didn't really want to, if she were honest with herself. Up here in the mountains, it seemed like a perfectly wonderful thing to do, staying close to him.

She felt more alive, somehow. More invested in the world. It was as if the cleaner air at this altitude was able to blow away the smog of her past. Her heart raced when he wrapped his hands around her waist to her closer.

"What if I don't want a status change?" she asked, thinking that she was crazy. Of course she wanted to change her status! She wanted...

Reid. She couldn't say much more after that because he kissed her. It started softly, barely there for a long moment. It was almost as if he were testing her, giving her the chance to back away. Did she want this? Yes! The resounding answer in her head caused her to pull his head closer.

That was the only invitation he needed. His arms wrapped around her waist, lifting her up slightly as his mouth covered hers. His head slanted as his lips moved over and over on her own. Automatically, she opened her mouth to deepen the kiss, her body tingling with the raw sensuality of his caress.

His response was to pull her closer, pressing his arousal against her stomach, which gave her a sense of power that she'd never felt before. She moved closer, sliding against him and heard his groan. Smiling, she felt an almost overwhelming need to hear that sound again, run her hands along those muscles that she'd been admiring recently, but hadn't had the courage to touch. Now she was touching, she was feeling and...yeah, he groaned again.

Her breathing was ragged, she couldn't seem to get enough oxygen to her lungs and rested her forehead against his chest. Thankfully, he was feeling the same way, if his heaving chest was any indication.

"We can't do this here," he murmured, his fingers sliding into her hair, ruining the neat and tidy braid she'd pulled her hair into.

"Why?" she asked, letting her fingers slide over his chest. He caught one of her hands, the deep rumbling in his chest telling her that just that simple movement was exciting him.

"Because if you continue touching me like that, we're not making it down off of this mountain tonight."

She stared up at him, not sure what he meant. He threw back his head and laughed. "You have no idea, do you?" he asked. He moved the hand he was holding until her fingers covered his erection, pressing urgently against the canvas of his shorts. "This is what you do to me, Selena," he warned her. "And if you continue to look at me like that, I'm going to encourage you to explore this in a bit more detail. On that rock right there."

God help her, she actually peered around his broad shoulder, considering the size and possible comfort of the flat, sun warmed rock.

"No," he laughed softly, pulling her head back to his. The kiss this time was softer but no less powerful. Thankfully, he lifted his head before it got out of control like the last one.

"Come on," he took her hand, helping her climb down. "I think we've climbed high enough for today."

"I thought we were going higher?"

He chuckled. "We will."

It took only about half as long to climb down the mountain as it had to go up because of the steepness of the decline, however they still had to walk slowly or they could trip and slide. That wasn't exactly how she wanted to get down off the mountain, so she listened carefully to Reid's instructions on descending. When she spotted his Jeep across the meadow field, her heart fluttered wildly.

Before she could step into the Jeep though, he spun her around, pinning her against the hood. "You realize where we're going now, right?" he asked, nuzzling her neck.

She gasped, shocked by the heat hitting her. "Where?" she asked, gasping when he nibbled a particularly sensitive spot.

"To my bed. Do you have any objections?" he asked.

"Fine. Just hurry up!" she gasped, shuddering when he found a spot that made her knees threaten to give out.

He deposited her in the passenger seat. As soon as he stepped into the driver's seat, he took her hand and placed her palm on his thigh. "I need you touching me, Selena," he groaned as he put the Jeep in reverse and pulled out of the parking lot.

It took less than forty minutes to get back to his house. Even so, it was still late afternoon when he pulled into the driveway.

By that point, she'd come to her senses, actually thinking about what they'd been doing on the mountain.

"Stop." He stepped out and looked into her eyes. "Dinner first," he announced. "You are probably starving after all that hiking, aren't you?"

Selena was relieved that she wouldn't immediately be rushed into his bedroom. "I am, but..."

"Don't even suggest that you can make something yourself," he warned her. "I'm sure my housekeeper has something ready to put into the oven. So come on," he walked around the car, closing her door as she exited.

When he saw the nervous look in her eyes, he shook his head. "Selena, if you don't want this, then say so. I won't pressure you." He moved closer. "But you should know that once I get you into bed, we're going to light the sheets on fire."

Seeing the earnestness in his eyes, she realized that he wasn't kidding. He really *did* want her. He WANTED her! This wasn't a fraternity dare. This wasn't a college prank that would be broadcast to anyone who might want the ridiculous, salacious details. Reid was attracted to her. To who she was. He wasn't going to push. Instinctively, she knew that if she wanted to go into the guesthouse and curl up under the covers alone for the rest of the night, he would let her.

That realization changed something. She didn't fully understand it, but she knew she wanted to experience Reid's touch. She wanted to feel him, to know him in ways she hadn't wanted to explore in a long time.

"I want this," she told him, feeling liberated.

This was Reid. He wasn't just gorgeous, sexy and incredibly appealing. He was intelligent, secure in who he was as a man, and a brilliant businessman. She wanted him. She might even lo...like him. And she definitely respected him.

She opened her mouth to tell him how much she wanted to make love with him, but the words came out wrong. "I'm not on contraception," she blurted, thinking back to that college night and her worries afterwards. Diseases had been the last thing on her mind at that point. A teenage pregnancy was her major worry. The possibility of a sexually transmitted disease had come later. Thankfully, the campus clinic had helped her through those traumatic tests and given her the reassurance of clean health.

His hand came up to her head, his rough fingers cupping her jaw gently. "I'll take care of the protection. No worries there. I don't want to rush you into anything."

She smiled, thinking that he was sweet in a dangerous kind of way. Yeah, all that raw power and intensity was right there, lurking behind his molten, almost glowing eyes. And all of that intensity was for her. He wanted her that much!

"Could we skip dinner?" she suggested, peeking up at him shyly through her lashes. She wasn't as hungry for food as she was hungry for him. For the way he made her feel.

"Damn, woman!" he growled and lifted her into his arms just as he had at the trailhead.

Laughing, Selena squealed as he carried her inside. "Put me down!" she laughed.

He rolled his eyes even as he took the steps two at a time, not even breathing heavily as he carried her up the stairs and shouldered his way into the bedroom where he lowered her feet to the floor.

Looking up into his eyes, her stomach muscles tightened with anticipation. "What are you going to do now?" she asked.

He stepped closer, pulling her hips flush against his own. "I thought I'd start with taking your shirt off."

Selena suddenly remembered that she was wearing an ugly sports bra. "Um...."

"Don't even try it!" he told her, chuckling and that sound...it was an amazing aphrodisiac! "I don't care if you're wearing lace or spandex," he told her, correctly realizing where her mind was going. "As far as I'm concerned, it's coming off too."

His attitude intensified her excitement and caused her to relax. It was a strange sensation, feeling both at the same time. If she'd had a moment to think about it, she'd say that they were opposite reactions.

Then he pulled her tee shirt off, dumping it on the floor without any concern, and she was too shocked to think of anything. She couldn't even protest.

Then his fingers moved to her breasts, his eyes tracing the path where her sports bra pulled her breasts in. "This isn't supposed to look sexy," he groaned, "but seeing your nipples through this material," and he ran a finger over each, causing her to gasp, "is pretty hot."

Over and over again, his forefinger teased that indentation, making her squirm and her knees to go weak. "Reid!" she gasped.

"I love it when you say my name like that," he told her, then did it again.

She grabbed his wrists, trying to pull his hands away. "No more," she told him.

His eyes lit up and he shook his head. "We're just getting started, honey."

Oh, she loved those sweet endearments! They sounded delicious to hear ears! "Could you hurry up?"

He laughed again. "No. I've been waiting a long time to do this with you. We're going to savor every moment."

She frowned, not sure she could take savoring this first time around. "Maybe we could savor later?"

His mouth covered hers in a kiss so hot, her toes literally curled. Her body couldn't stand the distance so she moved closer, her hands clinging to his shoulders as she pulled herself higher, needing a deeper kiss, wanting more. His hands tightened in her hair but the prickles only turned her on more, especially when he angled her head, deepening the kiss.

"I need more," he told her. "I want to see all of you."

With the heat burning from his eyes, Selena felt strong and powerful, beautiful. The way he was looking at her, surely it wasn't a lie," she told herself. This was real! This was what she'd been missing all her life.

With a quick tug of the laces, her hiking boots were tossed to the floor and she was relieved when he pulled the ugly socks off as well. They might have protected the skin of her feet from rubbing against her new hiking boots, but that didn't mean she wanted them on any longer than was necessary. He tossed the socks behind him with the boots and her shirt.

When his fingers moved to the waistband of her shorts, she panicked slightly, grabbing his hands to stop him.

"I won't take them off if you don't want me to, Selena," he promised. She still felt his fingers against her stomach. The sensation was startling, intriguing, and exactly what she needed to let him proceed further.

Gone were her shorts and then he was staring down at her cotton panties.

"Okay, I have to tell you...I was wrong."

She looked up at him, not sure what he might be wrong about.

"Those cotton panties...they're pretty hot," he shook his head even as he traced the simple elastic around her waist, before moving down to skim along her thigh. "I might like this." Then he shook his head again. "No, they have to come off." A moment later, they flew through the air over his shoulder. "One of these days, you're going to do a fashion show for me. I want to do a case study on the sexiness of the pieces Grace convinced you to buy and these cotton things." A moment later, he kissed the space just below her belly button. "Until then, I'll just have to enjoy every moment of the viewing and unveiling.

Selena couldn't help it. The laughter just burst out of her. When she'd first met Reid, she never in a hundred years would have used the term "silly" to describe him. But he put a lot of humor into everything he did, and this undressing process was simply one more example of that.

"You're…" she started to say something, but his fingers were tracing up the outside of her leg, then back again, this time on the inside. She gasped, arching her back as he came closer and closer to that heat between her legs. She was amazed by how wet she was and the man had barely even touched her.

"You're beautiful," he growled, his fingers moving along her thighs as she pressed them more tightly together. "Will you let me see all of you?" he asked.

She swallowed hard, her excitement warring with her nerves. "Why am I the only one naked?" she demanded.

He stood up and stripped, not bothering to put on a show. A moment later, he was completely naked. Gloriously naked. The man was built! Her breath caught as she came to her knees, her fingers itching to explore. "You're amazing," she sighed, caressing his chest, tracing the indentations where one muscle met another. There were so many ridges, so many bulges, and not an ounce of fat anywhere.

She was vaguely aware of his hands in her hair, but she was engrossed in her own exploration. Her fingers traveled higher, discovering that his pectoral muscles twitched as she explored them. Toying with his nipples, buried beneath a thatch of hair, made his fingers tightened against her scalp. It was the best reaction she'd gotten so she ran her finger over that spot again and again, just as he'd done to her earlier. His reaction was the same, a groan and a sharp intake of breath. Leaning forward, she let her tongue explore that nipple and his reaction was more intense.

A moment later, the slow exploration was finished. She found herself flat on her back, her hands held firmly over her head as he latched onto her nipple, his tongue lashing the sensitive peak before nibbling ever so gently. She pulled her wrists from his grip, grabbing his hair to pull his head away, but his deep chuckle gave her fair warning that he wasn't going to allow it. Sure enough, he reclaimed her wrists, pinning them more securely above her head and continued to torture her nipple. When she begged him to stop, he only moved over to the other. Selena was practically sobbing by the time he moved down her stomach, her body arching into his mouth now.

Thankfully, he had to release her hands and she grabbed his shoulders, unaware of how her legs had spread wide, making room for his hips. She realized their body positions when he moved even lower, his breath tickling the inside of her thighs.

A moment before she could protest, his thumb rubbed along her pink folds, spreading her wide. "You can't even imagine how hot you are, Selena," he told her. That was her only warning before his tongue began exploring her delicate flesh. His focus on that sensitive spot made her scream his name.

It had been so long since she'd been touched, and no man had ever done that to her, so when his mouth closed over her once more, one finger sliding slowly into her heat, her body splintered apart, throbbing with the beauty of her climax as waves of pleasure burst over her.

Slowly, he relaxed the pressure and pulled back, but only so that he could grab a condom from the bedside table. A moment later, he was back, looking down at her. She lifted her legs, feeling soft and fuzzy. "That was wonderful," she felt the blush stain her cheeks.

"We are nowhere near done yet," he promised, bending to kiss her. She tried to avoid his kiss, tasting herself on his lips, but he wouldn't let her get away. She kissed him back with everything she was feeling, all the turmoil and excitement, relief and gratitude. This was Reid and he'd just given her the most amazing gift. Something no man had ever taken the time to do.

Okay, so she'd had that one miserable experience in college and one boyfriend after that. Her boyfriend in her early twenties had been a fast and selfish lover. Never had she experienced pleasure from their time together.

Reid shifted her legs further apart, trailing along the insides of her thighs, making her shiver gently. Yes, she definitely wanted to feel him inside of her, but she knew that her part was finished. This next part, it was all for him. She shifted her hips, trying to help him as he pressed his way inside of her.

As he shifted into her heat, her eyes widened. The new sensations were...different from her past experiences. Suddenly, satisfaction vanished and the need returned! Stronger than before. Digging her nails into his shoulders, she moaned, surprised by the wave of sensation flowing through her.

"You okay?" he asked as he pressed deeper into her core.

"Yes," she whispered, gasping as he slowly filled her up. "More," she begged, licking her lips as she arched against him, trying to take him deeper still.

"Tell me if I'm hurting you."

She shook her head. "Just...more!" she pleaded.

But instead, he pulled out and she whimpered. "No!"

He slid smoothly into her heat. Deeper this time. Then out and she shook her head, trying to tell him to stop doing that. When he arched into her this time, she felt the friction and wrapped her legs around his waist, trying to pull him deeper still. "Yes!" she groaned, arching off the bed as she closed her eyes. "Too good," she sighed.

He pressed into her until finally, he was all the way in and she held her breath as her body adjusted to his size and girth. He was so big! So wonderful! She wanted to stay like this forever! "Perfect!" she whispered, unaware of the sight she made as he looked down at her.

Reid agreed. She was perfect. Beautiful, sensuous, glorious, and amazing!

But he couldn't hold back any longer. The way her inner muscles were squeezing, he was liable to lose control soon. Moving slowly at first, he tried to figure out the best way to move in order to give her the most pleasure possible, but it seemed that any way he moved, she liked it better. And that only made it more difficult for him to hold back. In the end, he reached down between their bodies, his thumb rubbing against that nub. He ignored her tugging at his wrist, enjoying the way her eyes widened. He knew she was close and sped up his pace, concentrating only on her pleasure, on bringing her to that pinnacle again.

When he heard her scream, he knew she was there. A moment later, her inner muscles contracted convulsively around his erection, which was all it took to bring him over the edge. Both of them came with a crashing pleasure that overwhelmed. He held still, feeling the last few pulses of her body as it wrapped around his and he groaned, feeling the sensations wash over him like a warm, erotic wave.

When it was all over, he rolled to his side, feeling like something had literally altered with the earth's atmosphere. His arms shook as he tried to keep himself from crushing her. Rolling off to the side, he kissed her shoulder, her neck, before pulling away.

After discarding the condom in the bathroom, he returned to find her curled up on her side, the comforter pulled over her as those beautiful blue eyes struggled to stay open. "Don't fall asleep on me yet," he warned as he climbed back onto the bed, pulling her into his arms.

With a yawn she tried to smother, she asked, "Why not?"

"Dinner," he told her, pressing a kiss to her shoulder. "You need dinner."

She smiled, but he could tell she was losing the battle to stay awake. "Later," was his only warning before those long, dark lashes closed completely.

For a long time, Reid watched her sleep, noticed the small freckles on her nose and cheeks, the elegant curve of her neck... things he'd never noticed because he was too entranced by those blue eyes of hers. With them closed, he could observe her more closely, see things that he'd missed while she was awake.

Selena was shockingly beautiful, even with those amazing eyes closed. He wanted to protect her and thought back to this morning. Bacon, he thought. And anorexia. He didn't know much about it, but he knew that it was a bit like an addiction. Wrapping his arms around her, he vowed that he'd never give her a reason to slip back into that way of thinking. Whoever had hurt her, he wanted to find them and beat them. Never an advocate for violence, Reid still wanted to teach the man who had hurt this delicate woman a lesson in respect.

Chapter 9

"This isn't going to work."

Selena turned towards the woman who had spoken. With a swift glance, she took in the pinched mouth, the overly made-up complexion, and the angry eyes. The assistant marketing director, Ruth. She'd been on vacation over the past week, so she hadn't been in on the brainstorming conversations. Now the woman sat in the meeting with a scowl, ready to criticize any and everything.

Pasting on a professional smile, Selena tilted her head. "I appreciate everyone's feedback. Why don't you think so?" she asked, folding her hands in front of her as she stood in front of the group. Unfortunately, her new boss, Dave, was in another meeting so he wasn't here to defend the group's efforts. After spending the night with Reid, making love to him and realizing how beautiful making love could actually be, Selena felt...empowered! She'd never felt this kind of euphoric happiness. A kind of serenity that not even Ruth's nasty comments and sneers could dissipate.

Ruth sighed as if the burden of this meeting was too much for her, then tossed the mock-up of the advertising board to the middle of the table with obvious disdain. "Because people don't buy makeup like this. They get one or two pieces at a time. Not an entire 'look' at once."

Digging deep for patience, Selena smiled. "I completely agree."

The woman rolled her eyes. Actually rolled her eyes! In a business meeting? That just...well, she supposed it happened but it was shockingly unprofessional.

"So, why would you even *suggest* promoting five different 'looks' to the public? It's a waste of advertising dollars that we could be spending on a more effective idea." She flipped through the financial reports, shaking her head. "I never should have gone on vacation. Dave should have run this by me before tackling such a ridiculous idea." She leaned forward, glaring at Selena. "What we've been doing so far has been working perfectly. Rembrandt Cosmetics has grown exponentially over the past decade. We were on the right course."

So much for her serenity! Selena counted to five before she responded. Then she lifted her eyes and focused all of her attention on Ruth as she said, "You're right. Rembrandt Cosmetics has expanded extremely well over the past ten years. And the current marketing strategy has advanced the product line and gotten the attention of many new customers." She paused, looking at the others. "I believe it is time to take the next step. Over the past year, I've listened and observed our customers, learning what they want, what they like, and how they shop. But more importantly, why they shop."

"Just so you know, customers don't go into a store and buy the entire line of makeup at once."

Selena told herself that Ruth didn't know of her background, didn't know that she'd been training the trainers for several years now. So she patiently nodded. "Yes. You're absolutely right. Sometimes. And sometimes, a woman needs a fast, efficient process to find out what works specifically for her. This idea does that."

"So, why are we here? If you know that women don't buy in bulk, this effort is wasted!" the woman sneered with a dramatic wave of her hands.

Selena brightened her smile, trying not to be patronizing. "Well, this idea does exactly what you're saying. I'm not suggesting that someone go out and buy an entire makeup line and Rembrandt definitely doesn't promote bulk sales. Every woman is different and every need requires specific attention. That's why we have very specific products for each look." She went back to the five pictures that she'd drawn when submitting her idea. "For the smoky eye, we're suggesting three different eye liners."

Another snort of disgust. "No one has the time to use three liners," the woman snapped, crossing her legs and turning her shoulders away.

"True," Selena continued. "The three different liners are for the different skin tones. A very pale woman can't use black easily. Not without going for the goth look." She paused while the rumble of laughter died down. "Someone with very pale skin should use a charcoal or brown liner. And a darker skinned person shouldn't use a soft brown liner. It wouldn't show up properly. She needs the darker tones." She picked up the papers that had been distributed to everyone at the beginning of the meeting. "Referring to the cost, there are three tiers, one for the teenager, who spends a bit more money but needs less expensive products. Another for the woman in her thirties who is still working to advance her career and is willing to spend a bit more money, but wants longevity in her products so they'll make it through the day without touch ups, and yet a third tier for the older woman who is more than ready to spend, but needs justification for spending money. Within each of those tiers, I've provided additional data on their spending habits, the product suggestions, the additional training required for each tier, and..."

"It won't work."

Selena surveyed the rest of the audience, knowing that they were on board with her ideas, enthused even, but none were willing to speak out against Ruth. Obviously, the spiteful woman wasn't the director, but Selena suspected that she was the kind of staff member no one wanted to confront directly. Acknowledging that, Selena knew that the woman was going to be a hindrance to progress.

It was essential that she get this woman on board.

For a brief moment, Selena thought about mentioning to Ruth that Reid wanted this marketing campaign. But saying that out loud brought back memories of yesterday and last night. Sleeping with the boss made her wary of bringing up his name. It felt… inappropriate.

Maintaining the professional smile, she turned to the others. "Does anyone else have any questions?"

They all shook their heads or sat in stony silence. "Ruth, perhaps you and I could meet, one on one. It would be easier to listen to your concerns and address them without wasting everyone's time."

Reid was disgusted. He'd been standing off to the side, listening and watching. He'd hired Ruth years ago as the assistant marketing director, but she had become an impediment to change. Well, any sort of change that she hadn't initiated, he realized. He'd always though that the woman was fiercely loyal. But now he was starting to realize that it might not be loyalty. It seemed more likely territoriality than loyalty to the company. The woman wanted to protect her territory and any change in the game plan, any change she hadn't thought up herself, was a threat to her turf.

He was incredibly impressed with how well Selena handled Ruth's objections. She was cool and composed, beautiful and professional.

Reid smiled, thinking about last night. She hadn't been cool or composed at any point during the night. Not even close. As soon as he'd touched her, Selena had been on fire.

Damn, he wanted her. Again! Would this overwhelming desire for the woman ever ease?

He hoped not.

Pushing those thoughts aside, he stepped fully in to the conference room. "I think that's an excellent idea, Selena." Everyone spun around, most with mouths hanging open in shock. He knew they were wondering which he would support, the new idea or Ruth.

"Ruth, how about if the three of us sit down and talk things over?" he suggested. As he watched, Ruth seemed to puff up with importance. Turning to the rest of her staff, she dismissed everyone with a sharp nod. Immediately, the others in the room stood up, gathered their papers, and filed out. A few of them nodded greetings in his direction, but most of them kept their heads bowed.

Reid took it all in with a glance and it angered him further. He didn't like any member of this staff being cowed for any reason. He and Brant prided themselves on running a corporation that valued individuals. Seeing his assistant marketing director in action, he saw clearly that she wasn't a team player and was sucking the life and enthusiasm out of the marketing team.

Ruth stood up, imperious as a queen, which fired his temper even further.

Even worse, Ruth wasn't willing to talk to Selena. Instead, she stood and, with her nose stuck up in the air, acting as if Selena weren't worth her notice, headed for the nearest exit. "Call my secretary and set up a time to discuss this. I'll help you refine these ideas to something more...appropriate."

Reid watched, tamping down his fury. He flicked his gaze towards Selena, trying to see how she was taking the abuse, but the hurt look in her eyes, a look she was valiantly trying to hide, only increased his fury.

"How about right now?" he suggested. His words might have formed a question, but his tone and expression were clear. It was a command.

And yet, she continued to try and play stupid power games. "I have another meeting, but we'll work this out, Reid. Selena has a decent foundation. Her ideas just need to be tweaked into something reasonable. Something that will appeal to our customers."

Reid shifted his weight, folding his arms across his chest. "I'm not sure you fully understand, Ruth. I like Selena's ideas. I moved her out here so that they could be implemented."

Ruth's smile faltered, but she rallied. "I understand that you want to help her advance her career, but her ideas aren't..."

"Her ideas are brilliant, Ruth. I have yet to hear a solid reason why we shouldn't move forward with them. Selena researched her ideas thoroughly. Every suggestion is backed up with both financial and consumer data." He leaned forward, bracing his hands on the conference room table, glaring at Ruth. "Either explain your concerns, backed up with solid research, or back off so that Selena can do her job."

He hadn't thought it possible, but Ruth's lips pressed even more tightly together. "The ideas aren't going to work, Reid," she snapped.

"Why?"

"Because they just won't!"

He frowned thoughtfully. "You don't want them to work because you didn't think them up yourself. Is that it?"

Her face went blank in surprise and he knew he'd hit it exactly on the mark.

But Ruth was nothing if not tenacious. "That's not the issue at all. I've accepted ideas from my staff and we've implemented them into the overall marketing strategy. We do it all the time. We're a team here!"

He saw the lie in her eyes. "If I asked members of your staff, would they agree with you?" he asked softly. He couldn't believe he'd missed Ruth's selfish machinations for so long.

Ruth stammered, understanding her jeopardy. "Of course they would."

"We'll see," he snapped. "That will be all."

Ruth wasn't exactly sure what to do. Instead of arguing any further, she picked up her notebook and walked stiffly out of the conference room.

There was a long silence while Reid considered his next step. Ruth would have to go. There was no chance she could stay on with the company. Not after that performance. But...

"I'm so sorry," Selena breathed from behind him.

He swung around, only realizing that he was still angry when he saw the concern in his eyes. Reid ran a hand over his face, trying to calm down. He'd missed something that had cost his company time, money, and creativity. He was furious, but with himself. "This isn't your fault, this is mine. I allowed an employee to become a tyrant in my own backyard. That's on me. I hate when I miss things." He pulled her in for a gentle hug. "But your ideas are solid, Selena. Don't doubt that for a moment."

She hesitated, but eventually her arms wrapped around his waist and he sighed into her hair. "I'll let you know what's happening by this afternoon, okay?"

Selena pulled out of his arms, thrilled to have his support. "Got it. And remind me never to get on your bad side," she teased as she gathered up the marketing materials she'd brought in for the meeting.

He laughed and she wanted to wrap the sound around her like a blanket, remembering it from last night while he'd made love to her. Goodness, that sound was...and she loved it. That sound was a precursor to something wicked and delicious.

Something occurred to her and she stopped with her hand

resting on the door knob. "You're not going to fire her, are you?" she asked.

He spun around, looking down at her. "Of course I am. She'll never support your ideas. I can't have someone inhibiting progress. In fact, Dave should have fired her years ago."

She bit her lip, trying to test out various possibilities. "What if she's right? What if my ideas aren't good?"

He pulled her in and kissed her. "Selena, if she were right, she would have had solid justification for her disagreement. As it was, she simply announced that the ideas weren't good. That's a sure sign of someone afraid of being overshadowed. So no, Ruth's rejection of your ideas doesn't concern me in the least. In fact, they confirm my opinion." His arms tightened around her for a moment. "Besides, I usually go with my gut when promoting an idea, but I back up my ideas with data." He winked at her. "Brant isn't just a pretty face. He might be an ass and the most annoying brother around, but he's pretty brilliant with numbers. He looked into your suggestions and agreed that it would work. He calculated that your ideas would bring in an additional twenty-three percent more revenue over the next eighteen months."

She relaxed slightly. "So..." Grinning, she recognized the look in his eyes. "You're not thinking about Ruth, are you?" she asked, using the poster boards as a shield, trying to defend herself against the heat in his look.

It didn't work.

"No. I'm definitely not thinking about Ruth and her tyranny over my marketing department."

She laughed, feeling an excited bubble burst inside of her chest. "You're thinking something naughty."

"Yes. You could definitely say that."

Selena shifted her materials. "I'm going back to my office."

"Don't you want to know what I'm thinking about?"

She shook her head and backed away from him, but she couldn't stop the silly grin. "No. I definitely don't want to know what you're thinking."

"Why not?" he teased, resting a hip on the conference room table.

"Because you've already admitted that it is something naughty. Whatever it is, the idea is going to distract me for the next hour."

"Just an hour?" he purred, lifting a dark eyebrow in question.

Selena shrugged slightly and headed towards the door. "Maybe longer." With a saucy turn, she glanced over her shoulder. "Maybe not."

The rest of the marketing team hadn't gone back to their offices. Instead, they were all warily waiting to see what happened after the contretemps in the conference room, positioning themselves around the copier and the kitchen, trying to look busy. But in reality, each and every one of them were nervously watching. Never before had they witnessed anything so dramatic, having been under Ruth's thumb for too long.

Selena knew they were anxious about their jobs. Were some of them actually sweating? Ruth in a bad mood meant she would start lashing out at the staff members.

So while their boss had exited the room furious, this new person...she laughed!

After that, two things happened. About half of the staff relaxed, knowing that it was better to get on board and support the new sheriff, while the others who aligned themselves with Ruth scuttled to their offices to update their resumes.

Selena stepped into her office, not surprised by the drama. In fact, she'd been expecting it, although not so publicly and she'd expected it last week when she'd first arrived and introduced her ideas. Change was always difficult and her idea took the marketing and training efforts in a completely new direction.

Unfortunately, as soon as she got to her office, she found that there were stacks of files with a note on top. "File in the filing room."

Ruth was making a power play. This was her way to keep Selena busy so that she wouldn't have time to get things done.

Selena glanced at her schedule, surprised to find a number of new e-mails. As she read the first few messages, she realized that her afternoon meetings had been canceled. There was no longer a meeting with the arts department, the graphics department, or the team that would be coordinating events for the advertising launch. Everything had been canceled.

"You look like someone just told you your water heater burst in mid-winter," a friendly voice came from her doorway.

Selena looked up, recognizing Gianna from Brant's office last week. "Hi there! How are you doing?" she asked, knowing that Gianna was also new to the company and struggling to fit in. She felt a kindred spirit with the gloriously beautiful woman with the lilting accent.

Gianna laughed brightly, dark curls dancing around her shoulders as she leaned against the doorframe. "I heard you'd just endured your first kerfuffle with the lovely Ruth."

Selena leaned back in her chair with a sigh. "I'm sure it will blow over." Gianna might be new and friendly, but Selena didn't want to start gossiping.

Gianna nodded and moved into the office, sitting down in the chair in front of Selena's desk. "Yeah, from what I've heard from others in the marketing department, Ruth never lets anything blow over. She's a bit of a despot around here."

Selena smiled, thinking that Gianna was right. "How have you dealt with her?"

Gianna, with her normal Italian gesture of dismissal, waved her hands in the air. "She's a boil on the heel of this world," the woman declared. "I ignore her."

Selena laughed, shocked and impressed with Gianna's description. "I'm not sure that's going to be the most effective answer since she's my boss."

Gianna's cell phone buzzed, indicating a message. She looked down at it and rolled her eyes. "The King has bellowed," she announced, hefting the phone as if she wanted to hurl it against the wall. "I don't understand American men," she muttered as she stood up. "They work all day, never taking a jiffy to simply enjoy life."

A secret smile formed on Selena's features as she thought back to her weekend with Reid. "Some of them are very good at enjoying life to the fullest," she replied, ignoring the woman's miss of the word "moment" versus "jiffy". It definitely added to Gianna's charm.

With a sound of disbelief, Gianna swept out of the office. But a moment later, she poked her head back in. "Don't give up! Your ideas are perfect! Keep fighting!"

Then she was gone and even the air needed a moment to settle.

Selena gathered the stack of files into her arms, determined to get the filing done. She couldn't ignore the pile, even if it interfered with her job.

But as she stepped out of her office, Dave stopped her. "Don't worry about that stuff," he announced, a satisfied grin on his handsome features.

"But Ruth left a note?"

Dave chuckled. "Ruth was let go a few minutes ago. She hasn't cleaned out her office, but she stormed out of Reid's office and was heard yelling at him."

Selena wasn't sure how to take that. Was it because of her? Had she...?

"The whole staff owes you a huge thank you. She has been terrorizing us for three years."

"Oh, well…." Selena had no idea what to say to that.

"Don't worry," Dave assured her cheerfully. He was certainly in a good mood! "We'll figure things out tomorrow once the dust has settled. But this means more responsibility for you. Since Ruth is gone, I'll have to step up. I'm not abandoning you, but you're going to have to take more of a lead on your idea." He touched her forearm. "I'll still be here to advise and steer the campaign. And the team is great. Just do what you think is right. We'll have regular meetings to discuss your progress."

Dave took the files and dumped them on an empty desk. "Come to my office. We'll brainstorm on the best way to move forward."

And that, apparently, was the end of Ruth's rule in the Rembrandt Cosmetics marketing department. As she stepped into Dave's office, her cell phone pinged. Looking down, every one of the meetings that had been canceled an hour ago was back on her schedule. People interrupted her conversation with Dave repeatedly, stopping by to say how excited they were about her ideas and offering suggestions.

Selena had no idea what happened, but when she was nibbling at her salad over lunch that afternoon, she overheard someone talking about Reid and how he'd pulled everyone into the conference room, telling them that he wanted them to come up with ideas, talk about them, brainstorm. There was no more dictatorship in this department and he was going to work hard to bring back the innovative culture.

After hearing that, her admiration for Reid's business leadership skyrocketed. A problem was presented and he handled it. The problem solved by the end of the day. And in the hours that followed, as Dave listened to every idea and offered encouragement, there was an almost tangible difference in the hallways. An excitement that hadn't been there before.

Chapter 10

"You're still here."

Selena looked up from the notes she'd been writing and smiled welcomingly at Reid who was leaning against the door of her office. "So are you, apparently."

He stepped in further. "I was waiting for you to tell me that you're ready to head home."

She relaxed, feeling the heat of his gaze on her. "I drove in today. No need for a ride home."

"Still, you have *other* things to do tonight," he pointed out, sliding the notebook away.

She smiled up at him. "You changed everything around here, you know."

Reid's returning smile was a bit slower. "I should have realized what was going on sooner." He lowered his head and kissed her. Just a quick kiss, but it sparked an almost tidal wave of desire inside of her.

"Are you ready to head out of here?" he asked, his voice husky and suggestive.

"Yes," Selena breathed, more than ready to take a break. She remembered Gianna's comment about how Americans work too much and, since it was already dark outside of her window, that wasn't a completely inaccurate point.

They drove home in separate cars, but Reid was right behind her the whole way. And when she stepped out of her car, he was there, pulling her into his arms.

"I have work to do tonight," she told him as he backed her up towards his house instead of allowing her to walk towards the guesthouse.

"Not tonight. Your work tonight is to let me make love to you. It's an incredibly serious assignment."

"I don't know," she sighed, holding onto his shoulders. He pulled her purse and tote bag off her arm and dumped them by the doorway, steering her into his house.

"Think I'm going to allow any kind of resistance?" he teased, bending to nibble along her neckline.

She smothered a laugh even as she pulled away, but he didn't let her get far. "I know that you're trying to get me upstairs to your bed so you can do naughty things to me."

He shook his head. "Nope."

That was startling news. "You're *not* trying to get me upstairs?"

He shook his head again. "Not going to happen."

"Why not?"

"Because you've been walking around the office in these sexy heels all day. I saw you walking towards the kitchen to get coffee, I watched you in the conference room, I noticed your legs crossed earlier as you listened to ideas from the graphics people...and I'm not going to make it to the bedroom." With that announcement, he lifted her onto the granite island in his kitchen.

By the time she realized what she was sitting on, he had her dress unzipped. "Reid!" she gasped, trying without success to wiggle away.

With a rip, her underwear was gone, tossed over his shoulder. "I can't wait to buy you more," he groaned sliding his hands up underneath the hem of her dress. The material moved with him and he smiled, but the smile wasn't friendly. And it sent jolts of awareness through her body.

"Lean back," he ordered.

She stared at him for a long moment, but then his fingers slid into her heat, teasing her and she gasped, jumping up slightly. "What are you going to do?"

His smile widened, as did the intensity of her anticipation. "Only things you'll like, promise. Now lean back," he commanded again. She didn't obey him immediately, her eyes closing ever so slightly as he slid a finger inside of her heat. She was shockingly wet already, obviously just as eager for his touch.

"Don't stop," she whispered, her nails digging into his shoulders.

"Lean back," he repeated, nibbling his way down her collarbone, "or I'm going to stop." To reinforce his threat, his finger started to slide out of her.

Automatically, she shifted her hips, silently begging him to continue. Her fingers curled, her breath caught in her throat. She was so close! He'd barely touched her but...just another moment and...

He stopped! Gasping, Selena opened her eyes, ready to scream at him for stopping when she was so close! "Why?" she growled, her legs tightening around his hips. "Please!"

"Lean back," he ordered once again, kissing her neck and her shoulder that was now bare since he'd pushed her dress down so it pooled around her waist. "Lean back and I'll give you what you want."

She whimpered, but understood that he wasn't fooling around. She glanced behind her, but he took her hands, lowering her back to the countertop. "It's cold!" she hissed, but he only chuckled.

"I'll warm you up in a moment," he promised. "Lift your hips for me first."

Feeling awkward, but her body zinging with the hope of a climax, she lifted her hips slightly. He quickly pulled her dress out of the way, before gazing down at her. She was naked other than the thigh high stockings Gloria had convinced her to purchase and the heels she'd worn to work.

He tweaked her nipples and whatever she'd been about to say was gone from her mind. His fingers slid down over her stomach, between her thighs.

"I love you like this, Selena," he groaned, his eyes following his fingers' path. "Do you have any idea how beautiful you look right now?"

"No. I know how much I want you to put your fingers back," she admitted, too desperate to be shy. "And I know you're teasing me." With that, his smile widened and he bent over her, his lips hovering over her nipple.

"You're right. I am teasing you. It's fun."

She writhed on the countertop as his mouth closed over her nipple, his tongue flicking the sensitive peak. "Reid!" she shrieked, her fingers diving into his hair. Her knees rose as she wrapped her legs around his waist, pulling him closer. He was still fully clothed, his tie tickling her belly as his lips teased her nipple.

"Reid, this isn't...I can't take much more!"

He laughed, his hands smoothing up and down her legs. "Oh, you're going to take a whole lot more, Selena. And you're going to love it!"

She shook her head, trying to sit up. But he stopped her, holding her in place.

"Going somewhere?" he teased, his fingers sliding into her wet heat again.

Selena froze, entirely focused on his fingers. "I need to...!" His fingers twisted and she arched her back, her hands gripping the edges of the counter.

"What do you need?" he asked softly, his fingers moving gently.

"That! Just that! Don't stop!" she sobbed, twisting her body

121

in an effort to make his fingers keep doing exactly what they were doing.

"You don't want this too?" he asked softly.

She couldn't open her eyes to figure out what he might do, so Selena wasn't prepared when his mouth closed over that sensitive nub. With just a few flicks of his tongue against that nub, she splintered apart, the pleasure so intense, she couldn't even make a sound this time. She wasn't aware of her fingers pulling at his hair or the way her legs tightened around his shoulders. Selena gasped for breath, trying desperately hard to melt into a puddle of desire.

"Let it happen," he soothed, his fingers moving expertly against her body, increasing the pleasure and then...slowly letting her body settle back, releasing the pressure as the climax subsided.

Gasping for breath, Selena fell back against the counter, unaware and unconcerned with the cold stone now. All she could feel was her body throbbing with the after effects of pleasure.

"Reid," she whispered, loosening her grip as he pulled away. She heard him shuffling and opened her eyes slightly. He was taking off his clothes. With a smile, she shifted, sitting up to better enjoy the show.

"Ready for another?" he asked, tossing his slacks over a chair, then turning to press between her knees before sliding her forward, his erection nestled between them.

"Yes. I think that would be lovely," Selena replied with a smile.

"Good." A moment later, he shifted, positioning himself at her opening.

"Now," she urged, wiggling to help him enter her. With a grin, he obliged and Serena felt him slide smoothly into her body. She arched her back, taking more of him, wanting him deeper still. Closing her eyes, her head fell backwards as her arms wrapped around his neck. "Yes!" she whispered, shifting a bit more to take all of him into her body.

When he was fully inside of her, he paused, taking a breath and she felt the warmth of him everywhere. Slowly, he started moving. Thrusting deeper and deeper, she dug her nails into his shoulders and let him take control. She couldn't lift her hips to meet his thrusts, not on the counter like this. But she tightened her inner muscles around him, needing him to go faster. When he did, she held her breath as each thrust brought her closer and closer to that pinnacle. And when he brought her over one more time, she tightened her legs around his hips as the pleasure rolled over her, taking all thought with it.

A few more thrusts and she felt him reach his own climax but she couldn't do anything to help him. All she could do was hold on.

Breathing. Heavy breathing and soft touches.

Smiling, Selena slowly loosened her arms from around his shoulders and pulled back.

"You doing okay?" he asked, as he lowered his head to kiss her. Selena realized that he hadn't kissed her until that moment and almost laughed out loud. All of that was just because of her shoes?

"I found a pair of killer red heels at the store the other day," she told him.

His whole body stiffened and she knew that he was picturing her in the red heels. "You're going to kill me," he groaned. "And I'm going to die a happy death."

Selena laughed, thinking that he was the most delightful man she'd ever met.

Chapter 11

Selena felt as if she were drifting through life on a happy cloud. She loved Denver. She absolutely loved marketing, but she ached to get back to the training rooms and connect with the sales representatives. Her first love would always be working with the ladies on the front lines. She had several ideas on how to help the company sell the new concepts too!

Even better than her new job and her new town...she was in love with Reid. Not the silly, schoolgirl crushes she'd experienced watching jocks in high school and college. Nope, this was a heart pounding, sweet, and terrifying feeling that made her sigh wistfully every time he came to mind. She didn't just enjoy the sex with him, she liked spending time with him. It had been two weeks since that momentous hike. Two weeks of coming home from work with him, making love with him, cooking meals, laughing and sharing her day with him. He was funny and kind, sweet and excitingly menacing when he got that look in his eyes. Every time he touched her, he rocked her world.

None of her previous relationships had done that for her. Selena recognized that her past relationships had all been one sided. The men had been with her for the sex and she was with the men to soothe that vulnerable, insecure girl inside of her.

Thankfully, she was over that now. This time, with Reid, she felt as if this was real, as if he needed her just as much as she needed him in her life.

"We going out to lunch today!" a lilting voice announced.

Selena looked up to find Gianna stepping into her office. The woman was too beautiful for words. In another life, Selena might have felt intimidated by Gianna. But the woman was just too friendly and outgoing. Besides, Gianna had decided that they were going to be friends. The spunky Italian bombshell didn't really give a person a choice. Everyone in the office seemed to go along when Gianna made a decision.

And since she was usually right, no one argued about her dictates.

Except for Brant, Selena thought. Reid's brother seemed ready to explode into a fury every time the lovely Gianna stepped into his air space. It was almost hilarious to watch. Selena even suspected that Gianna did things to provoke the very staid Brant on purpose, wanting to spark his temper in any way she could.

"You're stalling," Gianna announced and plucked Selena's pen out of her hand. "We must try that restaurant down by the art center. I haven't been there and someone said we couldn't get a table."

Selena's eyes widened with confusion. "Well, if we can't..."

"We get one!" she announced, her Italian accent coming out a bit more forcefully. Gianna certainly loved a challenge! "No one tells *me* that they don't have room."

Selena laughed but stood up, grabbing her purse. "Fine. If we can't get a table there, then there's that sandwich place around the corner. I've heard that it's good too."

"No!" Gianna announced, slicing her hand through the air in that way only Italians could. "We dine at the special place."

No arguments this time. There was a good chance that Gianna was right. So far, every man groveled at her feet. She had the eyes and the figure that made men drool, so who was she to tell the vivacious woman that they wouldn't be allowed to dine at the exclusive place?

"Let's go. I have heard about your effect on men. I want to see it in action." Selena hoisted her tote onto her shoulder and followed Gianna out of her office.

They were at the elevator when she spotted Reid coming out of an office further down the hallway. For a moment, she paused to admire him. He was so tall and handsome, so amazingly virile.

And angry, she thought. Interesting. She hadn't heard about any new issues lately.

Their eyes locked and her heart stopped for a long moment. She couldn't breathe, couldn't move. Vaguely, she heard the elevator ping, indicating that the elevator had arrived, but she couldn't tear her eyes away from him.

And then he was gone. An icy fear entered her heart as she watched him talk to someone on the floor.

"Ready?" Gianna asked.

Selena pulled her eyes away, blinking as she tried to re-orient herself. Elevator. Lunch. "Right!" she gasped and stepped into the waiting elevator. Gianna pressed the button that would take them both down to the lobby level, but Selena couldn't think about lunch.

What was going on? Reid had glared at her as if she'd done something horrible. Thinking through the morning, she couldn't think of anything that had gone wrong. The campaign's schedule was ahead of where they were supposed to be. There hadn't been any contentious meetings...what had gone wrong?

Or was she reading too much into the look? It had been only moments and in a crowded hallway. Was she imagining the anger in his eyes? He'd hidden the look quickly, then walked away. But...?

"Forget men!" Gianna said as soon as the door opened.

Selena blinked and looked at the shorter woman. "I'm sorry?"

Gianna laughed, the sound filled with the absolute joy of life. It was a sound Selena had only learned to make over the past week.

"Men aren't worth it, Selena."

"I'm not..."

"Reid Jones? The nicer brother to Brant Jones, my boss?"

Selena laughed but it sounded a bit too self-conscious. "Reid and I aren't..."

"Of course you are and it's wonderful that you are experimenting. Especially since you're doing it with the nicer of the two brothers."

"Three," Selena corrected without thinking about it.

Gianna stopped and glanced at Selena. "Three? There are *three* of them? Where's the third? I'll have be sure to avoid him too!"

Selena sighed, rubbing her forehead. "Um...I think that the third brother, Mick or Mack or Mike, something like that...lives out in the mountains somewhere."

"I've never seen this person!" she said with another wave that seemed to dismiss the man simply because she'd never met him.

Gianna continued, ranting about Brant and how serious he was, how emotionally uptight and annoying the man seemed to be. Selena listened with only half an ear while she tried to sift through possibilities for why Reid was so angry.

They arrived at the beautiful restaurant and Selena cringed. "Name on the reservation?" a blond woman asked, obviously not impressed with Gianna's wild curls or luscious figure.

"We don't have a reservation, but we'll take a table near the window."

Selena almost laughed along with the hostess. The window tables were usually the best in the house and reserved for the high rollers.

"I'm sorry, but those tables are all reserved. Perhaps..."

"Hello!" Gianna beamed, moving over to a man in a business suit.

Selena cringed, not sure who he was. Nor could she hear what Gianna was saying to him, but a moment later, the man threw back his head and laughed. A moment later, he lifted Gianna's hand to his lips, kissing her fingers in a very old-world manner.

"I think we can squeeze in two beautiful ladies for lunch," the man announced, glancing over Gianna's shoulder at Selena.

Selena winced inwardly, the insecure girl from high school rearing her ugly head. As soon as she realized what she was thinking, Selena stopped, her head tilting back slightly as she squared her shoulders. This was her world now. She didn't cringe about anything! Never again! The two of them might get kicked out of this restaurant, but they'd go with their head held high and with a story to tell later on.

But to her surprise, the man winked at Selena, his gaze taking in her figure with obvious appreciation.

"This way," he took Gianna's hand and tucked it into his elbow.

A moment later, they were seated at one of the best tables in the restaurant, looking out of a floor to ceiling window that displayed the beauty of the Rocky Mountains in the distance.

"Nice!" Selena whispered after the restaurant manager had walked away with a bow. "I don't know what you said, but I think you're a genius!"

Gianna laughed. "I'm glad someone appreciates my brilliance," she said.

"Uh oh," Selena chuckled. "Who doesn't appreciate your genius?" she asked.

Gianna rolled a shoulder as if dismissing the person who had dared to ignore her. "It do not matter," she announced. "He is unworthy of my attentions anyway."

Selena leaned back in her chair, admiring the woman. To an outsider, Gianna appeared to be one of those women who got everything she wanted simply by snapping her fingers. But Selena had gotten to know the brunette and had discovered that Gianna was gracious and gentle. She loved life, embraced it with both hands and wanted the rest of the world to be just as happy. There wasn't a mean bone in her body, unless someone was unfair to another person. Then watch out! Gianna's imagination would bring the world down around anyone who had dared to hurt another human being's feelings.

Just the other day, Selena had come around the corner to discover one of the managers berating his administrative assistant. Later that afternoon, the man had come out of the kitchen with a coffee stain covering the front of his dress shirt, muttering curses under his breath. When Selena walked into Gianna's office, the woman was carefully storing away a nail file, a satisfied look in her dark eyes.

"What did you do?" Selena had whispered, knowing that the spilled coffee was her doing, but not sure how.

"I grew up with brothers," she explained with a dismissive shrug. "I learned to get back at them in unexpected ways."

Selena had laughed and mentally vowed never to get on the woman's bad side.

She leaned forward, curious about Gianna's anger towards Reid's brother. "So you have a thing for Brant?" Selena guessed.

Gianna's dark eyes sparked and she let loose a slew of Italian that Selena didn't even try to follow. A few more violent hand gestures and then...calm.

"*Non e niente per me!*" she gushed. From Selena's knowledge of Spanish, which was similar to Italian, she figured out that Gianna was trying to convince the world that Brant didn't matter to her. "He is just my boss. Nothing but my boss and only because my father insisted that I come to the United States to gain more experience. Pah!" She took a deep breath, centering herself once again. "Besides, we are talking about you. And why you looked like a wounded animal moments before."

Selena wasn't sure what to say. Gianna was too perceptive and it made Selena uncomfortable. But Gianna's saving grace was that she genuinely cared. The beautiful woman wasn't asking just out of curiosity. The woman wanted to save the world, Selena thought. It was sweet.

"It really isn't anything important."

The waiter arrived. Selena ordered a salad with roasted vegetables and all sorts of interesting berries. Gianna ordered pasta with some sort of exotic cheese that sounded delicious, but Selena knew better. The sauce would be too heavy for her to feel comfortable during the afternoon. So she wasn't jealous in any way of the other woman's meal.

"So, what was it?" Gianna asked after the waiter had departed.

"You don't really give up or forget anything, do you?" Selena asked with a grin.

"Never!" she laughed, tossing her head slightly and all of her dark curls danced around her lovely features. "I'm like a dog with a..." she snapped her fingers in the air. "What's the phrase? Stick?"

"Bone," Selena corrected. "Yes. You are like a dog with a bone. You don't relent."

"Yes. A dog with a bone. You Americans have the most interesting phrases! I love your language."

"English?"

Gianna laughed and her eyes sparkled. "There's American English and British English. They are so different! Dramatically different and both are so fascinating!" Then those eyes narrowed. "You try to change the subject but I not let it work," she admonished. "What hurt your soul before we left? You looked like your heart began aching."

Selena laughed, shaking her head at the woman's perception of drama. "Nothing so horrible as that. I just thought I saw someone who was angry. And I wanted to know why."

"Ah, you are in love with our handsome leader! I thought so!"

Selena pulled back, horrified! "Reid? No! I'm not in love with him. I just...he looked upset and I..."

Another tilt of her head and Gianna asked, "Why would you be embarrassed by being in love? It is wonderful! Love is the fruit that gives flavor to life! It makes us smile and gives us pleasure!" She leaned forward conspiratorially. "If the man knows what he is doing, that is!" and she laughed, delighted. "Most men," another slice of the air, "they fumble and mess up. But I think that Reid, he never fumbles, eh?"

Selena had never had such a blatant conversation. "Um... well..." she couldn't stop the blush.

"Yes!" Gianna clapped her hands gleefully. "He is good! Reid gives you immense pleasure so he is a good man!" She sighed. "His brother is...not! I doubt that man knows the difference between a man and a woman!"

. "Do you mean Brant?" she asked, both horrified and fascinated. "Are you...?" she started off.

The waiter arrived with their meals and Selena paused, not wanting anyone to overhear their conversation. Reid and Brant were powerful men in the Denver business world and she didn't want any disparaging comments to float around about either of them.

When the waiter departed, Selena turned back to her new friend. "Are you and Brant...?"

"Having sex?" she finished bluntly. "Never! The man is a goon! He is a termagant! He is a..." she stopped, waving her hand in the air as if trying to find another word.

"Do you mean buffoon?" Selena suggested carefully, not wanting to tease Gianna for her use of the wrong word because she had a beautiful grasp of the English language. One hundred percent better than Selena's knowledge of any other language. Her knowledge of Spanish was basic at best. She'd taken French classes in high school and college, but because there wasn't any place to practice using the language, Selena had lost her knowledge over the years.

"Yes!" she nodded. "He is a buffoon! A stick in the dirt!"

"Mud," Selena offered.

"That too!" she said, pointing at Selena with her fork to emphasize her words. "An absolute stick in the dirt and mud!"

Selena laughed. "I never would have thought you would be attracted to a man like Brant Jones."

Gianna shivered. "Never would I be attracted to a man like that! He is cold and soulless!" She stopped, peering shrewdly at Selena. "And you changed the subject again."'

Selena covered her mouth, trying to smother her amusement. "I didn't really change the subject. You sort of went off on a tangent."

She leaned forward. "What is this tangent? I know not of this word."

"Don't worry about it," she replied. "You were talking about how annoying Brant Jones is."

"No! We were discussing you and your love for Reid Jones." She stabbed the pasta and spun the fork, twisting the pasta onto the spoon.

And...they were back. "I'm not in love with him."

"And yet, you are making love with him every night. I know this is true but your love is recent, yes?"

"Uh..."

"Yes! You've only been with him intimately for a week, maybe two." She smiled when Selena's mouth fell open. "I see the glow in your smile and you walk with a delighted bounce to your step now. Before...when I first met you, there was a sadness to you. A..." she snapped her fingers again. "A timidity. Is that the word? Yes! You were timid." She shook her head. "No. Timid means that you were scared. You not scared. You were...reluctant," she finished. "Yes. That is the word for you. Reluctant. Now you embrace life more!"

Selena stared at Gianna, stunned at the woman's ability to really *see* a person. "You're scary," Selena whispered reverently.

Gianna laughed, delighted. "That is not the first time I've heard that! Now speak. Tell me why you feel your man is hurt."

"Not hurt. I think he's angry about something. I'm not sure what's going on."

"Not with you," Gianna announced.

Selena wasn't sure. The look Reid had given her before they'd left had seemed personal. But perhaps she'd just caught his eye at the wrong moment and his anger had nothing to do with her. Selena knew that she had a tendency to internalize issues. It was both a strength and a weakness, and was a constant struggle for her.

For the rest of the meal, they talked about business and work stresses. Thankfully, their conversation steered clear of romantic topics.

When they returned to the office, Gianna went back up to the executive floor where her office was located and Selena moved down the quiet hallway to her own. But she couldn't seem to get Reid's angry scowl out of her mind.

Later that evening, she waited for him to come by her office and take her home. But darkness fell and he didn't come to her office. Since he'd driven her to work that day, she called a cab to get home, wondering what was going on. As soon as the cab pulled up to Reid's gorgeous house, her anxiety doubled. The lights weren't on. He wasn't home?

She paid the driver and walked around to the back, wondering what was going on.

"Meow!"

Selena felt Cat rub against her legs.

"I don't know where he is, honey," she bent down to scratch Cat behind his ears. "He didn't tell me anything."

"Meow!" he insisted, leaning into her legs and hand. "I know, little guy. It's confusing to me too."

Selena knew that the cat had food and an accessible pet door that allowed him to get into Reid's house. So Cat would be fine without Reid for the night. But Selena didn't like leaving the poor fellow alone. Cats weren't the solitary creatures everyone thought they were. Cats actually needed just as much attention as dogs.

"Okay. Why don't you come into my place?" she suggested.

Cat agreed and raced towards the door to her house, then looked back over his shoulder. "I'm coming!" Selena giggled.

Selena flipped off her shoes, sighing with relief as she dumped her bag and purse on the chair right inside the door. "Are you hungry?" she asked the cat, heading towards the kitchen.

She pulled out a can of tuna and gave some to Cat, then dumped the rest onto a plate for herself, adding lettuce, spinach, and some cottage cheese. Selena carried her plate over to the front window overlooking the pool. Reid's house was still dark. Where was he? Why hadn't he called?

Not that they'd discussed their relationship, she thought. What were they to each other? At first, she'd tried to keep their relationship friendly. He was her boss, after all. But he didn't want that. And in truth, she didn't either. Never had she felt such an intense connection with a man.

So, what were they to each other? As she stared out at the darkened house, she suspected that their relationship meant a whole lot more to her than it did to him.

And that hurt!

Selena tried to tell herself that this wasn't a repeat of the past.

It wasn't high school or college and Reid wasn't one of those insecure, horrible teenagers that needed to humiliate someone to make them feel strong. Reid was strong, powerful, and confident. He was...

Not here and she didn't know what to think.

She looked at her purse where her cell phone hid, thinking to send him a text message asking if he was okay. Or if she'd done something to annoy him. Besides that look right before lunch, she hadn't seen him since they'd driven in to the office earlier this morning, so how could she have done something wrong? Unless... had she messed up on the marketing campaign somehow? Had she...?

Selena stopped herself before she went down that rabbit hole. She'd done that too often in the past. Straightening her spine, she remembered her therapist's advice to not internalize everyone's problems as her fault.

If Reid was angry with her, then he needed to talk to her and tell her what she'd done wrong. Until then, she wasn't taking the blame for his bad mood.

With that in mind, she got ready for bed. Cat jumped up onto her bed, purring as he curled his body around into a ball and fell asleep on her lap.

For a long time, she petted the feline, enjoying his company even if Cat wasn't nearly as wonderful of a companion as Reid.

Unfortunately, she didn't see Reid for the next three days. He wasn't in the office and no one knew where he'd gone. Or if they did know, they weren't saying anything. In fact, Selena looked at the others in the office kitchen, thinking that there was a very odd silence among the staff members.

Chapter 12

"Eeeeeh!" Selena shrieked, jumping backwards. When she realized that the...thing...in front of her car door was just a dead mouse, she sighed, putting a hand to her chest. "Cat!" she grumbled, then turned and headed back into the guest house. And for the first time in three days, she didn't glance over her shoulder to see if there were lights on in Reid's house.

"I'm going to find a new place," she muttered as she pulled a piece of paper out of the garbage can and walked back outside. Carefully, she lifted the dead mouse that Cat had left her as a present. She dumped it into a plastic bag and then tied it up with a double knot.

"Meow!"

Selena shook her head as the adorable predator sidled up to her, rubbing his body against her legs.

"No!" Selena admonished the cat. "I'm not petting you. Petting you makes you happy and when you're happy, you kill things. I don't want you killing anything!"

"Meow!" Cat insisted.

Selena wasn't strong enough to ignore the plea. "Fine!" she grumbled, bending down to scratch behind his ears. "You know you're annoying, right?"

Cat's only response was to purr louder. "By the way, how do you get out of the guest house every night? You curled up by my side when we go to sleep, but..."

"I built a cat door to the guest house as well," Reid's deep voice said.

Selena froze. A sexy pair of bare feet came into her line of vision. Slowly, she let her eyes move higher. Jeans. Loose, soft jeans that hung around his lean hips, low enough for her to...oh my!

Ignoring the obvious erection, she stood up and brushed the cat hair off of her hands. "You're back," she observed. "When did you get back?" Bare chest! Damn, he was playing dirty!

He moved closer and Selena immediately took a step away from him, lifting her hand up to stop him. "Don't," she whispered and turned away.

He stopped, his hands falling to his sides. "I'm sorry, Selena. I wanted to tell you where I was, but..."

"It's fine," she told him, pulling back and forcing her lips to curl upwards into a smile. She wasn't feeling smiley today, but she didn't want Reid to know how badly he'd hurt her. "I'm off to work," she told him.

"Ruth filed a lawsuit against me for wrongful termination," he announced.

Selena felt a chill whip through her. Turning back, she looked up into his eyes. "She...?"

"She claimed that I'd fired her because she was a woman. Unfortunately, she has a powerful family and...well...my lawyers won, but it's been a long, difficult week. And I couldn't contact you Selena," he said softly.

"You couldn't text me and tell me that..." she started to say something sappy like, "Tell me that you were okay," but stopped herself just in time. Shaking her head slightly, she lifted her hand. "It doesn't matter. You don't report to me." She took a deep breath. "I have to..." she stopped again. Unable to stop herself, she looked up into his eyes. "Are you okay? Did you really win?"

"Yes. Of course," he replied, his eyes hard and unyielding. Selena watched him, wondering what it would feel like to live in his head, to know that the world would bow to your dictates.

"That's good. Ruth wasn't a nice person."

"No. My lawyers had been bringing staff members in to give testimony over the past few days. They couldn't say anything to anyone either. Not until the judge ruled. Which happened yesterday. Her claim was dismissed completely."

He'd been involved in a horrible, unfair lawsuit! He hadn't rejected her! He hadn't...

He hadn't bothered to even text her to tell her that he was alive.

Pushing her relief aside, she nodded calmly, keeping her eyes above his chest. "That's good. I'm glad. Ruth wasn't a good person."

"Selena..."

"I have to get to work."

"I couldn't contact you! I wanted to. But my lawyers warned me against saying anything."

She stopped him. "I understand, Reid. And you don't owe me anything. We had no understanding. You don't report to me. It's the other way around. You're my boss." She glanced behind him at the beautiful guest house and shrugged. "And my landlord. But..."

"No!" he growled, moving closer and taking her upper arms in his hands. "We might not have defined our relationship but you're a hell of a lot more to me than just an employee. And yes, I know that I shouldn't touch you *because* you are an employee, but..." he moved closer, "I can't seem to stay away from you, Selena. Even after the nightmare of the past week, I can't stay away. I thought about you every minute while listening to that evil woman's accusations. But every time I wanted to contact you, my lawyer stopped me, telling me that no one could know about this lawsuit yet. If any word got out to the media, there would be hell. The media wouldn't want the truth! You know damn well that they'd prefer Ruth's version of the story because it's more exciting!"

Yes, that was true. But it didn't address the issue hanging between them. "Reid, you don't owe me any explanation."

"I don't...!" he released her, throwing his hands in the air. He stepped back as he ran his hands through his hair, mussing up what was already a bit messy since he'd just woken up. When he turned back to her, her stomach tightened with that determined look to his features. "I'm not letting you go, Selena. There's something between us. You don't trust me, and I get that. I didn't call and I should have, even though my lawyers warned me not to. I should have called just to tell you I was okay."

"You don't..."

He lifted his hand and she pressed her lips together. "Selena, if you tell me one more time that I don't owe you anything, I'm going to..." he stopped, and readjusted his topic. "I owe you an explanation. And I owed you a phone call. We're..." Once again, he stopped.

Selena waited, wondering what he might say.

"We're lovers, Selena. And I know that means something to you so don't even try to deny it."

She opened her mouth, wanting to say he was wrong. She wanted to be a sophisticated woman who could have sex with a man and walk away with a smile the next day. But that wasn't who she was. She wanted the commitment. She wanted the long-term relationship. She wanted...Reid. She wanted the love and marriage and lots of kids. Cat needed a dog to snuggle with at night and needed someone else to leave...dead presents for!

"I'm fine," she lied. And with those words, she died a little inside.

Reid watched her carefully, looking for signs that she was

lying. His gut told him that she wanted all of the same things that he did. But...

There!

"Selena!" he groaned, pulling her into his arms. She was stiff for only a moment, then he felt her melt against him and he buried his nose in her flower-scented hair. "I need more than just a nice time between the sheets."

He felt her shudder and then her hands crept around his waist. Feeling her fingers against his bare skin was heaven and hell. He loved her touch, the way she smoothed out all of the roughness of the past several days. But her touch was also a bit of hell because he knew that he had to get into the office. He'd had only two hours of sleep last night after leaving his lawyer's office. Andrea was a legal shark and he admired her ability to win. But they'd been up until the wee hours of the night strategizing, coming up with a way to keep Ruth from coming at them from another direction. Around three o'clock in the morning, Andrea and her team had come up with ten different legal filings aimed to stop Ruth from speaking out and creating a publicity nightmare. Ruth might have lost her wrongful termination case against Rembrandt Cosmetics, but that didn't mean she couldn't sully the company's name in the media with her accusations.

So Andrea had filed several counter-suits against Ruth. The papers would be filed first thing in the morning which would require Ruth to remain silent while the other lawsuits worked their way through the court system. One of Andrea's legal team had a gag order ready for a judge to sign this morning.

It had all moved so fast. Andrea was brilliant and effective, but exhausting!

"I don't know what we have together, but let's figure it out, okay?" he asked, pulling back to look into her eyes.

He could see the indecision in her eyes and wanted to pull her back into his arms, carry her up the stairs and make love to her. But he had to get back to his lawyer's office for more meetings and he only had about ten minutes until he needed to leave. "Can we talk about it tonight? I don't know what time I'll be done, but I'd like to see you."

Selena debated back and forth, obviously arguing with herself mentally. But in the end, she was just too fair of a person to ignore his request.

"Fine. Tonight," she stepped out of his arms. He chuckled when she reached down and scratched Cat, then slipped into her car. Damn, she had mighty fine legs, he thought as she pulled them into her roadster. And her black heels looked...amazing! He couldn't wait to have her in his arms tonight. Maybe he'd ask her to take tomorrow off so they could make love and get everything settled between them. He didn't want her living in the guest house any longer. He wanted her in his house. In his bed. Every damn night!

"Tonight," he repeated. "I might need to work late again, but I'll find you, okay?"

"Okay," she replied tonelessly and pulled the door closed. A moment later, he watched her drive away, wishing that he could ignore his responsibilities and just make love to Selena. He wanted to make her feel good, to show her in the most basic way that he wanted her in his life.

Damn, he was messing this up! Never before had he wanted a woman to be in his life. Never had he felt such an overpowering need to...well, to just be with a woman. He wanted her so badly, and not just sexually. He wanted all of her. He wanted her heart and soul. He wanted...

He wanted her love. Hell, he realized that he was in love with Selena! What a hellish time to realize that he'd finally found that elusive thing that everyone raved about, the thing that he'd thought he'd never find.

Somehow, he'd have to show her how he felt and hope that she might feel the same.

Chapter 13

"Andrea, I don't care anymore," Reid said as he walked down the hallway.

He wondered if the blond woman next to him ever ran out of energy.

"Well, for now, she's stopped. But we'll continue to monitor her case filings. If anything else comes up, I'll let you know."

Reid pressed the button for the elevator. "I want you to sue her for the money she's caused me to spend on all of her frivolous lawsuits," he decided. He suddenly realized that Andrea was an extraordinarily beautiful woman.

But she left him cold. He had no interest in the woman other than for her brilliant legal mind.

She smiled, nodding her head. "A suit for abuse of process was filed at nine-thirty this morning. We're asking for my entire team's legal fees, plus punitive damages of five million dollars. We won't get that much, but I put in an amount that should dissuade her from using her family's money on someone else without the resources that you have. She's abusive, Reid. And I'm going to stop her."

Reid laughed, shaking his head. "I should have known you'd be on top of it already."

Andrea grinned and, in a rare moment when the lawyer let her guard down, she flung her hip out, her hand fisted on top and smiled. "Yes, you should have!" He was shocked to see that her smile literally transformed her features. The shark went from a stunning beauty to almost a lovely, impish elf.

He threw back his head, laughing as the elevator opened up and he stepped inside. "Sorry for doubting you, Andrea."

"Don't worry. I'll take care of the last few details."

"Good. Call me if anything else comes up."

She was already turning away, heading back to her office by the time the elevator doors closed. Reid suspected that Andrea was already thinking about the next issue. Did the woman *ever* sleep? He doubted it. She seemed to exist on coffee and...work. The woman didn't have anything else going on in her life.

Glancing at his watch, he muttered a curse. It was after midnight. Damn it! He'd texted Selena earlier in the evening, letting her know that he was still planning on talking to her. But at the time, he'd thought he'd be done five hours ago.

He drove back to his house and parked the car. As soon as the lights turned off, Cat raced around the corner of the guesthouse, rubbing up against Reid's ankles. Bending down, he scratched the little guy's back, hearing him purr. "Hey buddy. Were you all snuggled up with the lady?"

Cat didn't reply, too happy to have attention.

"Yeah, you're a sucker." With one more pat, he stood up and headed for his back door. But at the last minute, he heard the door to the guesthouse open.

There she was! Selena looked...hot! The tee shirt fluttered around her upper thighs. There were no lights on in the guest house and her hair was mussed. Had she been asleep?

Walking over to her, he had a thousand things he wanted to tell her. But as soon as he reached her, all he could do was pull her into his arms and kiss her. Just one kiss, he thought. One kiss and he'd tell her what she meant to him, how he wanted to define their relationship. But that one kiss led to another. And then another.

He lifted her into his arms, carrying her back to her bedroom. He was vaguely aware of Cat curling up on the chair.

Clothes were torn off. Bare skin. His hands cupped her breasts and it wasn't enough. Their breath mingled together as they strained, frantic to make up for the past three nights apart.

"Hurry!" Selena gasped, handing him a condom. "Reid, hurry!"

He would have laughed if he could have slowed down. But he couldn't. Not even a little!

"Bedroom," he groaned as he rolled the condom down his painfully throbbing erection. He hadn't even taken off his clothes. Selena had just unzipped him and released his shaft.

"No time!" she told him.

He agreed. With a flash of brilliance, he lifted her into his arms. Pressing her against the wall behind her, he wrapped her legs around his waist. "Hold on, Selena. Just..." he closed his eyes and tried to be gentle, but three days without her was three too many.

"Now!" she gasped, wiggling against him as she tried for the same goal.

So instead of slowing down, which he didn't think he could accomplish, he lowered her down, impaling her on his shaft. As soon as her tight, wet heat surrounded him, he groaned, burying his face against her neck.

"Move!" she ordered, grinding her hips as her fingers tightened in his hair. "Move, please move!"

He might have responded. Reid wasn't sure. In his mind, he laughed, but his body was too close to the edge and he needed to feel her climax. He wanted that more than he wanted his own release. So he moved, shifting his body and using the wall behind her for leverage. Thrusting in and out, he pushed her closer and closer. Normally, he would use his hands and fingers to help her to the edge, but his hands were busy holding her butt liked where they were. Besides, he could feel her body tightening, getting closer and closer. She looked wild and beautiful and...then she shifted again, her body frantically reaching for that release.

When it came, he knew and tried to make it better for her. But the way she was moving against him, plus her inner muscles clamping down around his shaft, he couldn't hold back. The release was powerful and it took only two more thrusts before she was screaming his name.

Silence. He moved slightly but her already relaxed body stiffened with outrage that he would dare to move after such a perfect experience.

"Just a moment longer," she whispered, her lips grazing his ear. Just that touch and he hardened again, ready for another round. What was it about Selena that just got to him so intensely?

She felt his reaction as well and pulled back, a soft, lazy smile to her beautiful features.

"Aren't you exhausted?" she asked softly.

He could smell the mint on her breath and the subtle perfume that was all Selena.

"Obviously not," he replied, shifting to nuzzle her neck.

With that, he carried her to her bedroom and started the whole process over again, but much slower this time. And more thoroughly.

Chapter 14

"Selena, here are the..." Gianna stopped in the doorway to Selena's office, a startled expression on her face.

Selena turned around to face her friend, unaware of the smile already on her features.

"You made up!" Gianna exclaimed, clapping her hands. "What happened? Did he apologize? Was he contrite? Did you make him beg?" She dropped into a chair. "Oh, men should always beg when they've done something wrong!"

"Gianna!"

Both women jumped when they heard the deep voice call out. But while Selena's shoulders jerked with surprise, Gianna's slumped as if she'd just been denied a treat.

"Master calls," she whispered.

In other circumstances, or if Gianna had been talking about someone other than Brant Jones, Selena might have laughed. But since it was Brant Jones, Reid's brother and the second owner of the company, Selena kept her mouth shut, stunned that the gentle, vivacious and, apparently, fearless Gianna would poke the bear in such a way.

The bear in question was furious. A moment after his bellow, the handsome and furious chief operating officer appeared in Selena's doorway.

"How can I help you today?" Gianna asked, standing up and turning to face her boss. "Do you have yet another pointless report you need me to build for you? Or perhaps I could do a bit of data entry? God forbid, you actually use my brain for something important!" she snapped. And with that, she swept out of Selena's office with a flip of her hair.

Watching from the sidelines, Selena realized that Brant looked just as stunned as Selena felt, but both of them remained silent. Selena watched carefully though, noticing that the man didn't take his eyes off Gianna until she turned the corner.

That's when he turned back to Selena, fury twisting his normally handsome features. "I apologize, Selena. Gianna isn't usually so..." he glanced back down the hallway, shaking his head. "Just...I apologize."

Selena took pity on him. "You know she has a master's degree in international business, right? Her undergraduate work was a double major in economics and finance. She really *can* do a lot more."

There was no change to his features but, for some reason, Selena suspected that he was startled by her news.

"Right. Well, she won't bother you again."

"Gianna isn't a bother in any way. In fact, she's helped me figure out several problems, recreating the marketing budget to help us find different ways to work in the extra features we want for this new campaign."

Again, there was no change in the man's features, but Selena knew that he was absorbing that information.

"Right." Without another word, he walked away, barely taking the time to nod in her direction.

Selena turned back to her computer and sent a message to Gianna. "Lunch?" was all it said.

The reply was immediate. "Yes!"

Selena felt bad that she was struggling with the tedious tasks that Brant assigned. Her friend was stuck generating low-level reports that didn't challenge her intelligence in any way. And most of the tasks took about an hour out of the eight hours she spent at work. The rest of the time, she moved from department to department, asking others how she could help them. She'd even done some legal work and found candidates for open positions for the human resources department.

Gianna might appear flighty and sexy, but she was intelligent and ambitious.

Unfortunately, Gianna hadn't had time to help with Selena's personal issue. And that was Reid. They'd spent the night together again, making up for lost time. But by the time her alarm had gone off this morning, he was gone, although he'd left a note on her fridge asking her if she was free for dinner tonight.

They'd talk and, hopefully, work things out.

Chapter 15

Reid froze, staring at the big man sitting in his leather chair. "What the hell are you doing here?" he demanded.

The man swiveled around, tipping his sheriff's hat back slightly. "A little birdie told me that you were messing up your love life big time," Mack said. "I thought I'd come watch the show."

Reid rolled his eyes and moved closer. "Brant needs to mind his own business," he grumbled, then enveloped the gruff sheriff in a bear hug. "How have you been little brother?" There was nothing "little" about Mack Jones. He topped both Reid and Brant by about an inch, but the three brothers were about the same in the muscle department. Reid and Brant honed their muscles in the gym during the weekdays while Mack worked out in the mountains, doing activities that would make most people shudder. Repelling down mountains, then climbing up seemingly sheer cliffs and over boulders.

Mack laughed at his brother, returning the hug with interest before moving over to the hidden fridge and grabbing two beers. "Better than you, apparently."

Reid texted a message on his phone, then accepted the bottle of beer Mack had opened. "I'm doing just fine. No need to worry."

"Not according to Brant. He mentioned you'd..."

Brant burst into the room. "Damn! Did hell freeze over?" he asked, then hugged his brother.

"I'm here, aren't I?" Mack teased. "So obviously, it's frozen solid."

They always teased their youngest brother that hell would freeze over before he'd venture into the city. Mack was the sheriff of a small town up in the Rocky Mountains. He loved his town and its quirky characters, and he protected them as if they were his bear cubs. He was equally protective of his mountain, helping the park rangers enforce the rules with the tourists that flocked to the woods every year. Didn't matter what the season, there seemed to be someone getting lost or doing something stupid in the mountains.

Mack didn't have to work. If he wanted, the man could sit back and relax while living off of the massive income he earned from the dividends from his stocks in Rembrandt Cosmetics. Mack had given his brothers his life savings to help them finance the company years ago. But he loved his job and enjoyed protecting his town and his mountain.

"So who is going to save your mountain when someone decides to camp in the wrong place while you're here?" Brant laughed, grabbing another beer from Reid's fridge and popping the top.

"They'll have to fend for themselves for a while. I heard that my big brother was screwing up a good thing."

Reid turned to look at Brant, an eyebrow going up, silently asking, "What the hell did you tell him?"

Of the three men, Reid was the most outspoken, Brant was the coldly controlled one, and Mack was laid back and relaxed. But people who knew the three of them understood to never underestimate any of them. They were all powerful in their own ways. Reid manipulated the business world. Brant controlled a financial empire by not just running the financials for Rembrandt Cosmetics, but also investing the brothers' money and making them all disgustingly wealthy men. And Mack controlled his town and his mountain. No one messed with any of the Jones brothers, except for their sister, Giselle. That woman could give as good as she got. And the brothers teased her unmercifully whenever she and her husband visited. Well, whenever she wasn't around her new husband, the Crown Prince of Altair.

Reid didn't want to think about what their baby sister and her husband did at night. Because she might be furious with their taunting and teasing each evening, but by the following morning, she was all smiles and happiness again. Whatever Jaffri was doing, Reid didn't want details, but accepted that the big brute made his sister happy, so...whatever.

"I'm not the one you should worry about," Reid announced.

Brant tensed and Mack, always observant, turned his laser focus on his brother. "What's going on in your world?"

"Not a damn thing," Brant grumbled. "Mind your own business."

"Ah, now that sounds interesting," Mack replied, leaning back. The more relaxed Mack became, the more one needed to worry. "So, what's her name?"

"I don't know what the hell you're talking about," Brant replied. "Don't you have a bear to save or a hippy to arrest?"

"All in good time. Hippies don't move that fast and the bears are out catching fish and fattening up. I have time to hear about whatever is making you angrier than your normally bitchy self."

"I don't..."

"Her name is Gianna and she's an Italian spitfire that pisses him off every time he walks down the hallway," Reid filled in.

Mack chuckled while Brant glared.

"Really, big bro? We're going there? Should we bring up the lovely Selena?" He turned to Mack. "He flew this woman out from Washington, D.C. to start a new marketing campaign. It's brilliant, but she had trouble finding a place to live. So, guess where she's staying?" he said.

Mack chuckled. "I've already swung by the house. Apparently, there's a woman who loves shoes sleeping in my bed."

That got Reid's attention. "You didn't...!"

"Relax, big brother," Mack replied. "I'm an intelligent fellow and figured out what was going on. My stuff is in the room down the hall from yours. And I fed your cat too. What's up with that? I thought you hated animals."

Reid relaxed now that his brother had assured him that Selena's privacy was intact. "The cat sort of...well, he showed up last winter and looked starving and pathetic. I fed him."

Mack threw back his head laughing. "And he never left, did he?"

Reid shrugged, trying to brush off his brother's amusement. "He and I coexist. And besides, Selena likes him."

"Who is this Selena I keep hearing about and how did you mess things up?"

Reid shook his head, taking a long swallow of his beer. "I didn't mess anything up. I'm going to marry her."

There was a long silence after that announcement as both brothers stared at their oldest.

"You're kidding!" Mack finally said, breaking the silence.

"Not even a little," Reid told both of them. Six months ago, the mere mention of marriage or love would have had Reid ending the relationship. But with Selena, he couldn't wait to get his ring on her finger. "I love her. She's..." he thought about last night and all of the nights he'd spent with her snuggled in his arms. Their early morning runs. The way she made him smile. Or the way she could walk into a room and make the world seem...right. Brighter. More interesting. "Amazing," he finally finished.

Mack and Brant continued to stare, but their attitude didn't bother him at all.

"Well, I'll be damned!" Mack said, then shook his head. "Congratulations! When do I get to meet her?"

"Not for a while. You're going to have to stay with Brant this visit."

"Too noisy at your place?" Mack teased.

"Don't go there. Not..."

Mack lifted his hands in defense. "Sorry, Reid. I understand."

After that, the brothers decided to change the subject, talking about their sister and what she might be up to, the number of times she'd been in the news lately for a project she was sponsoring in Altair. The women married to the men of Altair were vocal proponents of many worthy causes, their sister included.

Chapter 16

Selena stretched happily and slipped out of bed. They'd come back from the office last night and he'd immediately taken her into his arms. That had been the end of any discussion. But they'd gotten the most urgent lust out of their systems and he'd already gone downstairs to start making something for breakfast. She wanted to exercise before they ate, needing to stretch her muscles a bit. A swim sounded like the perfect solution, especially since Reid was throwing a big party for the media blitz this afternoon.

Selena pulled on her bathing suit, then grabbed a towel.

Padding barefoot towards the stairs, she smiled, thinking about that time he'd made love to her on the counter.

"You ready for this?" a deep voice asked. Brant!

"I can't believe that she did this!" Reid growled, his voice a furious hiss.

Selena sighed as she stalled on the top step of the staircase, listening to the two brothers and wondering if she should just head back to Reid's bedroom. Brant intimidated her. Selena knew that there was tension between Brant and Gianna, but Selena had no idea why!

Reid was nothing like what she'd thought of him originally. He wasn't like the other men in her past. He was warm and wonderful, passionate and fabulous! She loved him so much, it almost made her heart ache.

She should tell him, Selena thought, her fingers tightening on the bannister. She should just tell Reid how she felt about him, let him know that she had no expectations about the future, but tell him that she loved him. She should thank him for being more. More than the superficial, corporate ass that she'd originally thought him to be. More than the pleasure seeking frat boy she'd assumed he was as she'd peered at him through her pain-distorted lenses several weeks ago.

He was brilliant, gentle, kind, generous, full of laughter, and loved life like no one she'd ever met before. He embraced challenges. Thrived on them! It didn't matter if it was a mountain, a river, or a boardroom, he dove right in and figured out how to overcome any obstacle. Whether it was a new marketing plan or stopping an evil, disgruntled ex-employee, he fixed the problem with zeal and brilliance.

Selena chuckled to herself, shaking her head as she realized that she didn't just love the man. She admired him. Boy, he was a potent combination of power, lust, passion, and laughter! What woman wouldn't fall in love with him?

Thankfully, he used his power for good, not evil.

Looking at the beautiful stairs, the gleaming wood, she took a deep breath and banished her past. Reid was important.

She needed to banish her insecurities and embrace what Reid was offering.

And get ready for this shindig! Glancing at her watch, she realized that she'd have to hurry up if she was going to get a workout in. Too much to do and not enough time, she realized.

Skipping down the stairs, she pulled the towel closer around her, trying to cover the soft swells of her breasts revealed by her bathing suit. By other's standards, the suit wasn't particularly revealing. But by her standards, she felt practically naked.

Stepping into the kitchen, she pasted a bright smile of greeting on her face, wanting to make a good impression on Brant only because he was Reid's brother. Otherwise, she wouldn't care about the man at all. He was a cold, emotionless man who frustrated Gianna, enough of a bad endorsement in her mind.

Of course, she wasn't going to hurt Reid's feelings by being rude to his brother either. The two men were close. And there was that pesky detail about Brant Jones being her boss.

Yeah, she really hated having to remember those details.

"Good morning!" she called, hoping that her voice sounded happier to their ears than it did to hers.

"Good morning, beautiful," Reid grinned, turning and snaking an arm out to pull her in for a kiss. "Sleep okay?"

Selena's smile faltered as she put her hands on his shoulders, shyly glancing over at Brant who looked like an angry, mean statue with his arms crossed over his chest and glaring at her as if she were about to stab Reid with a fork.

"Um..." she pulled her eyes away from Brant and focused on Reid. "Yes," she replied, awkwardly smiling up at him and running a hand over his chest slightly. "Yes. Very well, thank you."

"So formal," he teased as he bent his head to nibble along her neck. "Ignore my rude brother, Selena. He's just grouchy because he didn't wake up with a beautiful woman in his arms like I did."

His voice was soft and low, and Brant most likely didn't hear Reid's words, but Selena still couldn't handle this conversation in front of others. It smacked too vividly of another time in her past. A time when...another handsome man bragged about "bagging" her to his friends.

"I need to go," she whispered back, pressing against his chest.

Reid sighed but relented. "Fine. But I'll be watching you."

Eventually, she was going to learn to stop blushing when he said things like that, but she wasn't there yet. Especially when she knew he'd be watching her body. Not her, per se.

"I thought you had things to do to get ready for the barbeque this afternoon?"

"It's all being catered," he reminded her. "I just have to be here for the deliveries this morning, then the event coordinator is taking over."

"Must be nice," she teased, thinking about how hard she'd worked the last time she'd entertained back in Virginia. She'd cooked and baked for days before everyone arrived, and the day of the party, she'd been on her hands and knees, cleaning everything from her kitchen floor to toilets.

"You'll find out," he told her and gave her another quick kiss before patting her bottom. "Go work out and then we'll get out of the way and let the experts handle things, okay?"

She smiled, glanced over at the still-scowling Brant, and moved away. "Will do," she told him, thinking she should probably head into the office to let him do whatever it is that rich men did right before an event like what he'd planned this afternoon.

With another self-conscious glance towards Brant, she turned and headed out to the pool, relieved to be away from his scowling disapproval.

Reid watched her leave and wondered if she would ever open up and tell him why she was so hesitant to embrace what they both felt. She was achingly lovely and yet, every time he pulled her close when someone else was around, he could feel the stiffness in her body. Hell, sometimes she was pulling back, wary of him even when no one else was around!

And yet, the moment he kissed her, she melted in his arms, became a wildly abandoned lover. He knew that she enjoyed being with him, and not just in bed. When they were alone together, she was relaxed and seemed happy to be with him. But he knew that she was holding something back. Something painful.

He had no idea how to help her share what was bothering her.

Probably because he'd never felt like this about another woman before. She was...amazing! Smart. Sassy.

Maybe that was what bothered him so much. She didn't expect a damn thing and yet, he wanted to give her everything. He searched for and found the ring that he'd bought a week ago. It had been in his pocket the whole time. He wanted the ring on her finger! He wanted everyone to know that Selena was his woman! She was completely oblivious to the way other men watched her, lusted for her! They saw her beauty as a prize, something to win and own.

They didn't see the gentle spirit underneath the killer body or know the warm kindness behind her welcoming smile. Others didn't know how much fun it was to simply sit on the couch and watch a movie with her, feel her soft curves as they melted against him. She was...amazing!

"You know she's gone, right?"

Reid blinked, not registering the words. "Huh?"

He turned to face his smirking brother.

"You've been staring at the door for the past few minutes as if she's about to walk back in. She's gone. In the pool now."

Reid glanced at the door again, wishing that she would walk back in. He wanted to be out there swimming with her, feeling the water swirl around them and watch the water slide down her impressive...

"Stop it!" Brant growled, punching Reid's arm. "You're in love with her. I get it. But stop mooning over her! It's pathetic."

Reid glanced at his brother, then threw back his head and laughed. "You're just jealous," he jabbed. "I know that you're mooning over that cute financial analyst. Don't even try to deny it."

His brother pressed his lips together, not denying anything. "You're an ass," was all he would say.

"And you're just as love sick as I am so don't even try it."

Again, no denial, but Brant's scowl deepened.

A knock on the door interrupted their brotherly chat and Reid smacked his brother's shoulder. "She'll be here at the party, right? It will be the perfect opportunity for you to talk to her outside of the office. Maybe she'll be a bit more receptive to your dubious charms when she doesn't have a spreadsheet in front of her." He walked out of the kitchen, but called back from the hallway as he went to answer the front door. "Even better, Selena is good friends with your little woman. And since I'll be hanging out next to Selena the whole time, you'll have a good excuse to corner your raven-haired beauty and find out why she hates you so much."

Reid was almost to the front door, but he heard his brother grumble, "I don't need an excuse and she doesn't hate me." The grumbling, as well as the implication that his brother was struggling with a woman, was so unprecedented, caused him to laugh harder. Damn, life was good!

Chapter 17

Selena pulled herself out of the pool, feeling incredible! Swimming laps definitely used different muscles than going for a run or taking a spin class, she thought. Her muscles felt good and the coolness of the water kept her from overheating. What excellent exercise! If she'd known how nice it was to swim, she probably would have joined a gym that had a lap pool a long time ago.

She picked up the towel and carefully dried her hair, thinking she probably needed a stronger conditioner if she was going to swim more often. The chlorine definitely caused the ends to dry out. She saw movement in the house and realized that the catering crew had arrived and were setting up. She didn't want to be caught out here in just a bathing suit, so she wrapped the towel around her and padded barefoot back inside.

At the door to the kitchen though, the deep voices stopped her cold.

"Damn, what a gorgeous rack!" she heard Brant say.

The deep laugh made her whole body freeze. "Yeah. Hard to find a rack like that. Impressive, right?"

Both men laughed and she could imagine Reid shaking his head. "Just another piece of meat. Need to keep that in perspective and not lose my head."

That cold sensation inside of her turned to ice. He wasn't talking about her, was he? She glanced down, realized that the towel had slipped, revealing her breasts in the bathing suit. Impossible! Reid had never been so crude before.

Shrinking back, horrified that he would refer to her breasts as "a gorgeous rack", she tried to find some other explanation. Reid wasn't like that! Nor had he ever treated her as "just another piece of meat"!

"I saw the way you were watching out the window a few minutes ago," Brant teased. "I noticed the way you were drooling."

Reid snorted, almost as if he were trying to dismiss his brother's comments. "As if you weren't drooling?"

"Yeah, but I prefer to call it salivating instead of drooling. Drooling seems so juvenile."

Reid chuckled. "Right. Like we're not acting like complete juvenile idiots over a piece of meat! Get over yourself. We're both ready for a taste. No use denying it."

She pulled back even more, disgusted by the possibility of Reid offering to share her. He wouldn't! He was jealous when some other guy even looked at her! Why would he offer to share her with his brother?!

Impossible!

And yet, those words were so similar to what she'd heard years ago. She shouldn't be surprised, but she was. Selena was horrified and disgusted. Reid had always treated her so sweetly, always acted like a gentleman.

But that was the way men operated! She knew from painful experience that men like that didn't think of women as individuals with hearts and souls. They considered women to be conquests. Hadn't she just been thinking about Reid as a man who liked a challenge? Someone who thrived on overcoming obstacles?

Well, she'd been a small obstacle, hadn't she? Or maybe she'd been a big one! She clutched at the towel, trying to hide her body as the old insecurities came rushing back. In her mind, she wasn't standing in the beautiful stone covered patio of Reid's lovely home. She was back in the frat house, the smell of stale beer and dirty socks surrounding her, making her gag as she listened to the fraternity brothers mock her. And worse, they were throwing empty beer cans at the guy she'd just given her virginity to the previous night. His laughter echoed once again in her mind as "fat girl" and "pathetic conquest" filtered back. Words she'd tried so painfully to banish from her mind.

As she stood there listening to Reid and Brant refer to her as "a piece of meat" and discuss the tastiness of her, all of those insecurities welled up, almost choking her. No longer was she the head of a new and innovative marketing idea, ready to launch her ideas onto the cosmetic world. She was the overweight, insecure college girl who had gone into a frat house thinking that the guy who had invited her had genuinely liked her. That he was willing to overlook her chubby thighs and round stomach. She'd smiled happily that night as she'd entered the dubiously-sacred hallways of the frat house, nervously searching for the guy who had invited her.

This wasn't happening! Not again! She pulled away, stepping back and almost tripping over her own feet as she tried to hide from the pain lashing at her heart. No! Reid wasn't like that! And yet, he and his brother continued to joke about different "pieces of meat", how one was just the same, it only mattered how much careful attention was put into the care of the meat, into the preparation.

He was talking about her! He was just like the others! Only, this time, there weren't any dirty socks stinking up a corner of the room. And she didn't smell stale beer or hear the ribald laughs of the others.

Just two men. Two grown men who she should have known better to trust!

A man like Reid wouldn't genuinely be interested in a woman like her!

Stop it! Selena heard the words in her head and forced her mind to stop. She wasn't ugly and it didn't matter if a woman was fat! Every woman had worth! Every woman deserved the dignity of honesty and respect!

Nothing was wrong with her, she reminded herself. It was the men who were wrong. It was the pathetic, insecure, disgusting boys who thought that women were a conquest.

No, she wouldn't go through that emotional turmoil again. She wouldn't starve herself as she had after that event. She wouldn't put herself at risk. Selena knew she had an eating disorder. Just as any alcoholic had to guard against the triggers that might set them off to drinking again, Selena had to watch for triggers that would cause her to start starving herself, from regaining control of her world by not eating.

Years of therapy had gotten her to this point. She was happy and healthy now. She was in control by being strong and confident. Selena was not going to starve herself again.

Lifting her head and straightening her shoulders, she pulled in a deep breath and slowly let it out. Closing her eyes, she did the mental exercises over and over again, reminding herself of her affirmation. She was strong and powerful, smart and worthy of her own respect.

This would not pull her down.

When she opened her eyes again, she felt better. More balanced. Yes, her heart still ached because she'd trusted Reid. Had fallen in love with him. But this was just life, she told herself. This was what other women learned early on in their dating lives. Selena just had to learn to deal with heartache later since she had avoided dating for so long.

This was just her journey. She'd hurt for a while...maybe a long while, but she'd get over this.

Walking over to the guest house, she let herself in, walking to the bedroom where she used to sleep. Until Reid had convinced her...until he'd fooled her.

No longer a fool, she told herself and stiffened her resolve, unaware of the tears spilling down her cheeks. When she saw her reflection in the mirror, she saw them and wiped them away. Silly to be crying over a man unworthy of tears.

And yet, he'd fooled her! He'd been so sweet and gentle, so kind. He'd made her laugh. Maybe that was the worst part of this, she thought. The way he'd made her laugh. And trust him. Yeah, she'd grown to trust him and that hurt. Because it took her so long to trust and yet, he'd gotten under her defenses. His sweet words and his teasing challenges.

Hunting through the drawers, she realized that all of the pretty underwear that Reid had teased her into learning to love was up in his bedroom. She'd literally moved in with the man! Good grief!

Enough! She dropped the towel and grabbed a pair of white, cotton underwear. They were perfect, she thought as she pulled them on. Walking away from the mirror, she ignored how uncomfortable the cotton felt against her skin. In just a few weeks, she'd fallen in love with the soft, slick feeling of silk and satin against her. She loved the way the lace cupped her breasts. And yeah, she'd loved the way Reid looked at her when he'd peeked under her dresses or shirts to discover what she was wearing underneath.

That was over. She could never be with a man who thought of her as a piece of meat. Or worse, a man who was willing to share her with his brother. She snorted as she opened the wardrobe to find something to wear. As if she'd allow a man to treat her like that! She wasn't the kind of woman who enjoyed being passed around! More power to women who enjoyed that kind of thing, but she wasn't one of them!

She reached for one of her regular dresses. But her fingers brushed the wardrobe bag containing the sundress she'd bought specifically for this event. Hesitating, she debated wearing the dress or just slipping into one of her old standbys. A sheath dress would be perfectly acceptable.

But the floral sundress with the slit in the skirt, hidden by a long ruffle...she remembered trying it on in the store...the spaghetti straps, the cinched-in waistline, the long, deceptively demure skirt...

If she'd been looking in the mirror, she would have seen the evil glint in her eyes. No, she wasn't going to wear a black sheath dress. First of all, the black would be too hot. And secondly, did she really want to shy away from a challenge? Reid thought he'd won by seducing her. Just like...No!

She was a different person now and she would never cower as she had in college. She would stand tall and proud. No more tears! At least...glancing at the clock, she realized that she didn't need to dress for another several hours. The media and models weren't scheduled to arrive until five o'clock tonight.

In the meantime, this was her opportunity to do something she should have done weeks ago.

She grabbed an old pair of shorts and a tee shirt. Slipping on a pair of sneakers, she hesitated. Her purse and keys were in Reid's house. She'd dumped them right by the front door where she normally put them.

Not a problem, she thought with determination as she pulled her still-wet hair into a messy bun, unconcerned with the bumps and ripples since she hadn't combed it out first. She didn't care about makeup either. She had things to do and not a lot of time to get them accomplished.

Stepping out into the bright sunshine, she wiped her eyes again, wishing she had a few slices of cucumber to take the redness away. But no matter. She wasn't stopping. Reid and Brant were probably out of the house anyway, off doing whatever it was that horrible men do when someone else was cleaning their house. God forbid the man actually clean his own toilet! He probably didn't even know how!

Why it was so important that the man learn to clean a toilet... well, she wasn't sure why it was important. Perhaps it was simply another example of how the man had an entitlement complex. He felt he was entitled to seduce any woman, even if she didn't want to be seduced!

Okay, that wasn't fair. Selena knew she'd gone into this relationship with her eyes open. She knew exactly what she was doing. If she hadn't wanted to be seduced, then it wouldn't have happened.

Take responsibility for her own desires, she thought with finality. She'd wanted sex with Reid. She'd wanted to fall in love with him. It was just the right time in her life for a romance.

She'd gotten it. In spades! But now that his true colors were showing, she wasn't interested. He was a demeaning, disgusting jerk who thought it was okay to share her, to objectify her and treat her like...like a piece of meat.

No more!

"Good swim?" he called when she slipped by his office.

"It was great!" she called out, smiling stiffly in his general direction as she turned and headed up the stairs. Two hours ago, she'd felt like this was her home. She'd started to feel comfortable here. Now it felt odd to walk up the stairs without his permission even though more than half of her clothing was in his bedroom and her cosmetics were in a drawer in his bathroom.

She'd get everything later. Once she had a place to put them, she reminded herself. And even if she couldn't find a place, she'd move into a hotel before spending another night here.

Something else occurred to her. Revenge dress, she thought with relish as soon as she spotted her purse and keys. Grabbing both, she hurried back out of the bedroom, not even glancing towards the bed for fear of the memories causing her tears to start flowing again.

It was over. Nice while it lasted, but over!

Hurrying out, she raced down the stairs, gripping the bannister so she wouldn't trip and fall. That would be the ultimate indignity, she told herself.

"Hey, Selena...?"

"I have to go," she called. He was still standing in the doorway to his office, looking amazing and virile. He was all of that, she knew. And a petty, juvenile jerk.

"Wait..."

"Can't wait!" she called with a wave.

"Selena!" he yelled.

She cringed slightly, hearing his anger. And there had been confusion in his eyes a moment ago as well. Bracing herself against such a look, she hurried out the door, ignoring him. She couldn't stop. Couldn't slow down. If she did, there was a high possibility that she would yell at him, reveal what she'd overheard, and she couldn't let him know how much he'd hurt her! No way!

That would be her secret to deal with. Her wounds to heal.

And the next man she trusted...if she ever trusted a man again... he wouldn't be an ass! He wouldn't think of a woman as "a piece of meat"!

Slipping into her Miata, she revved the engine and backed out. It shocked her to realize how much time she'd spent with Reid. They'd been driving to and from work together every day and, since his car was nicer and Reid preferred to drive, they always took one of his vehicles.

Now, driving away in her sporty car, she remembered how much she loved to drive. She'd really missed this over the past several weeks.

She drove down the driveway, ignoring Reid standing on the front sidewalk, his hands fisted on his lean hips frowning. Why in the world would he be angry?! The man had no right to be angry! Of course, he didn't know that she'd overheard his demeaning conversation with his brother. Reid had no idea that the truth of his disgusting personality had finally reared its ugly head.

Well, no more! She'd extricate herself from his clutches and move on with her life. Step by step. The first thing she needed to do was get out of his house. She wouldn't allow herself to live in his guest house. She was finding her own place to live, doing it on her terms.

Driving through the streets of Denver, another thought occurred to her. She'd lived here for several weeks now, but since Reid did most of the driving, she hadn't learned how to get around town.

Didn't matter, she told herself as she made another U turn before spotting the sign to get onto Highway Twenty-Five North. Speeding onto the ramp, she joined the mass of traffic heading out of the city. Heading north. Most of these people were probably heading towards the mountains and she gazed longingly at them in the distance. Beautiful, she thought. The snow-capped mountains were elegant and rugged, never letting a person down with their magnificence.

Unlike other people that she'd thought were so solid and trustworthy!

She spotted her turnoff, remembering it from the last time and turned left. Five minutes later, she pulled into the parking space right in front of the rental office. Getting out, she didn't care that she looked a mess.

"Hi there. Remember me?" she asked of the salesperson.

Obviously, the woman did. The wary expression in her eyes spoke volumes.

"Don't worry," Selena soothed her. "My...friend isn't here and I'm ready to rent. I don't care about his issues."

The woman's mouth opened and closed. "I'm sorry, we don't have any two bedroom apartments currently available. I rented the last one last weekend. We have studios and one bedrooms."

Selena's smile widened and she wondered if she looked a bit crazed since the saleswoman stepped back slightly, as if she were cringing in fear. "Perfect," she replied, ignoring the woman's reaction. "I want a one bedroom, with a washer and dryer in the unit."

The salesperson typed in a few things on her keyboard, her eyes moving over the monitor before she nodded. "I have two available. One looks out to the mountains, but it's a bit more expensive. The other looks down onto the courtyard. It might be a bit noisier on the weekends," she warned.

Selena thought about those options for a long moment. She briefly considered taking the apartment by the courtyard, just to irritate Reid since he was so adamant about the pool parties and happy hours being a hookup event. But in the end, she knew that she'd be happier with a mountain view apartment. It would be glorious to wake up every morning and see the mountains off in the distance.

Another good thing about Colorado. One could actually *see* in the distance, even during the summer months. The humidity and pollution in Virginia diminished the view of the Shenandoah National Park, a part of the Appalachian Mountains. There was also a great deal of light pollution, so even at dusk, it was sometimes hard to see with the city lights making the distance fade away.

But she was here now. And she loved it! Colorado seemed to feed her soul in ways she hadn't thought possible.

Although, she'd thought that about Reid just this morning.

More fool her.

Selena walked behind the now-bubbly salesperson who discussed a litany of the various stores and conveniences that were close by. Once in the apartment, Selena was surprised at how small the apartment felt, but perhaps that was to be expected after living in a twenty-five hundred square foot guest house, or Reid's six thousand square foot house. Going from that grandeur to an eight hundred square foot apartment was...well, it would just be a change. Everything in life changes, she reminded herself. This was simply another change. Another challenge.

Looking around, the white walls and oak cabinets weren't much to fall in love with, but she'd figure out how to make this into a home. Something cozy, warm, and welcoming.

Then again, she had been working long hours over the past several weeks while planning all of the details for the marketing campaign. And things were going to get crazy again once this campaign got underway. The press was going to love her ideas and all of the social media blitz that would come along with this type of change in advertising would be a welcome distraction from dealing with Reid.

The salesperson was standing in the apartment, awkwardly shifting from one foot to the other, not sure what to say next.

"I'll take it," she told the woman.

Thirty minutes later, she'd signed the one year contract on the apartment, accepted her parking sticker and keys, then walked out. Taking a deep breath, she tried to feel good about this move. She should feel empowered and in control.

But deep down inside, in that place she didn't want to open up yet because she knew it would hurt too much, she could feel the pain just waiting to break out.

Not yet, she told her previously-scarred heart. "One more thing to do," she whispered. Getting back into her car, she drove back into the city. Luckily, she found a parking space not too far from her destination. When she stepped into the store, Selena was immediately greeted by Grace and her warm smile.

"Hi again! Back for more?" she asked, moving to shake Selena's hand.

Selena blinked back more tears. "Yes. I need something special for an event tonight. I don't want to wear the plain strapless bra I'd originally purchased to go with the dress. I want something spectacular," she explained.

Grace smiled, her eyes twinkling with mischief. "I have something that would be perfect," she said and walked towards the back of the store. Selena followed, feeling exhilarated. Princess Diana had stepped out in public in a daring, strapless black dress on the same day her husband admitted to an affair. This would be Selena's grand event in the same way.

Grace lifted a bustier into the air, holding the silver lace piece of art up for Selena's inspection. "How about this?" she offered.

Selena looked at the bustier, her smile increasing as she imagined what she would look like, and feel like, in the gorgeous piece. What was better, Reid would never see it. Oh, he'd know she was wearing something different, something enticing. But he'd never get even a peek. It would be her secret.

Her own "revenge dress".

"Why don't you try it on?" Grace suggested.

Selena agreed and moved into the plush dressing room, refusing to remember the last time she'd been here. When Reid accompanied her.

Taking a deep breath, she pulled her tee shirt and bra off, and slipped the bustier on. As soon as she secured the small hooks in the back and turned to face the mirror, she knew it was perfect! The deep V of the top would allow her to wear the sundress lower than she'd originally planned. And the boning in the construction would push her breasts up higher. She could just imagine Reid looking at her breasts.

"Yeah, I've got quite a rack," she whispered in satisfaction to her reflection in the mirror.

With a shake of her head, she pulled it off and dressed once more. Stepping out, she caught Grace's raised eyebrows and nodded. "I'll take it," she told the woman.

At the cash register, she cringed only slightly at the three hundred and fifty dollar price tag as she handed her credit card over to Grace. Revenge was expensive, she realized.

Didn't matter. Stepping out into the sunshine, she lifted her face, absorbing the warmth. What had started off as a wonderful victory had become nothing more than hours to endure until she could escape. Glancing at her watch, she realized it was later than she'd thought. She'd skipped breakfast and lunch, and her stomach grumbled. She thought about just not eating, but knew that wasn't a good option. Not with her history. Skipping meals lead to hunger and hunger led to either binge eating or...a more devastating reaction. No, she'd never go down that route again.

Instead, she stopped by a sandwich shop and grabbed a bite to eat, but was only able to stomach about half of it. Better, but she still grabbed a banana and nibbled on it as she drove back to Reid's house. She'd have to pack before the party. And somehow get her suitcase into her car without Reid seeing her. She wanted to be ready to hit the road by the time the party ended.

Possibly, she owed Reid an explanation, but she wasn't feeling benevolent at the moment. She wanted to hurt him. Not that it was truly possible, she realized. Hurting Reid was difficult since he didn't have a soul. No man who treated women the way he had earlier today could have a soul.

So, why were tears streaming down her cheeks as she pulled into the driveway? Parking her car behind the garage, she walked as quickly as she could into the guest house. Reid must have been watching for her though because as soon as she rounded the corner of the garage, he called out to her.

"Selena! Where have you been all day?"

She lifted the silver, tissue stuffed bag into the air, rushing to the guest house. Away from him. "I'm going to get ready. I'll see you later!"

He stopped, his eyes moving to the bag, then to her face. When he saw the redness around her eyes, he started towards her again. "What's wrong?"

"Nothing!" she called back.

"Then why are your cheeks red?"

A hand came up to her cheeks and she cursed herself. So much for looking cool and composed. "I guess I got a bit too much sun while running errands," she told him. "I really need to get ready. I'll see you in less than an hour," she called back.

Thankfully, he didn't follow her into the guest house. Once she was inside, she hurried to the back, hiding from him. When she didn't hear the door open and close, indicating that he really was giving her a bit of privacy, she leaned her head against the wall and tried hard to pull herself together again.

"Time to get this 'gorgeous rack' in gear," she whispered to herself.

When she opened her eyes, she was startled by her appearance. Her cheeks were definitely red and blotchy. Plus, her hair looked like a rat's nest! It was dry now but, since it hadn't seen a brush yet today, the strands were going every which way.

Shower. Makeup. Dress. Get over Reid. In that order.

She could do this, she told herself as she pushed away from the wall.

An hour later, she put the finishing touches on her makeup and reviewed her look in the mirror. She'd chosen to go ultra-romantic for this night's events. The floral dress and the soft, pink lipstick, the subtle eye shadow and smoky liner did the trick.

With a nod of satisfaction, she turned around and...

"You look beautiful," Reid was leaning against one of the wooden armoires.

Selena's determination quivered slightly as she surveyed him in the well-worn jeans and casual shirt. It was tucked in this time, showing off his lean waist and what she knew to be rock hard abs.

"What happened earlier today?" he asked softly, moving towards her.

Selena panicked, lifting her hands to stop him. "No!" she gasped. At the startled look in his eyes, she softened. "Please, I don't want to ruin my makeup."

He moved closer, his large, strong hands resting on her hips. "That never bothered you before," he commented.

She pulled out of his arms before the sweet embrace broke down her newly built defenses. "I've never had a string of journalists, models, and others all ready to listen to the new pitch either."

He grabbed her wrist when she tried to walk around him. "Selena, something is wrong. And it's more than just nervousness about tonight, isn't it?"

She looked up into his eyes, astonished that a man as insecure and horrible as to refer to a woman as "a piece of meat", could be so shockingly sensitive.

Perhaps he was just a sociopath underneath all of those muscles, she thought. A sociopath knew how to mimic emotions, but never truly feel them.

"I need to get ready for tonight," she repeated, staring at him, silently telling him that he needed to leave.

Reid stared at her lovely features, red and swollen with tears. What had happened? Was she angry about the morning? No, he was sure that she'd enjoyed their morning just as much as he had. Was she upset that he'd kept her in bed too long?

No, that couldn't be it. He might have initiated their morning activities, but she'd been an enthusiastic participant. Besides, she'd gone for a swim afterwards. He knew how important exercise was to her and admired her for that. Hell, he enjoyed a good workout everyday too. But no, this wasn't about exercising. She was assertive enough to tell him what she needed in that area.

No, this was different. The way she held herself, almost as if she might shatter if she moved...!

"Selena," he said softly, "tell me what happened, please?"

"I just have a few more things that I need to do to get ready," she told him. And with that, she turned away and slipped into the bathroom, closing the door firmly behind her.

Reid stared at the door for a long moment, wanting to open it and demand that she talk to him, party be damned. He couldn't lose her! Not now! Not when he'd finally realized how important she was to him. Hell, he was looking forward to having her on his arm tonight, to showing the world that he was her man. She was so incredibly beautiful and charming and...and vulnerable. He'd forgotten that part because she hid her vulnerabilities so well.

Her past. He still didn't know what had happened in her past, but he knew that whatever was bothering her had to do with the issue from her past. The issue that had been so traumatic, that she'd tried to destroy herself with anorexia.

Damn! He wanted to pull her into his arms and tell her that

he'd protect her from whatever was hurting her! He wanted to beat the crap out of whoever had hurt her feelings.

Turning away, he stormed out of the guest house, furious that she wouldn't talk to him, but not giving up.

Looking around, he noticed that the cleaning crew was packing up. The catering crew had placed the tables around the pool, the event coordinator was directing the other vendors. Vases of flowers were carried around to the tables, the smell of ribs grilling permeated the air, and the bartenders were stocking the tubs that would hold iced beer. There would also be circulating cocktails, but those would be prepared in the kitchen.

Ignoring all of it, he walked into his house, prepared to get ready so that he would be outside to greet the guests. But he discovered Brant and Mack lounging on his couch, laughing about something.

"Why are you here so early?" he demanded, looking at both brothers who wore almost identical dark slacks and white shirts, open at the collar.

"To annoy you. Why else?" Brant claimed, then clinked his beer bottle against Mack's as they chuckled.

"I will call Giselle and tell her that you guys are annoying me," Reid warned. "She'll fly out here with her entourage and drive both of you nuts trying to figure out what's wrong."

Obviously, the threat wasn't dire enough because his brothers just laughed. Rolling his eyes, Reid walked up the stairs, ignoring them so that he could get ready for the damn party. He'd wanted this to be a big bash, something that could highlight all of the work Selena had done to prepare for this campaign. But now, he just wanted it to be over so that he could talk to Selena and find out what or who had hurt her feelings.

Twenty minutes later, he walked back down the stairs, showered and freshly shaved, ready to greet his guests. He'd chosen khaki slacks, but a white shirt like his brothers. What he was wearing didn't matter though. He was eager to see Selena.

Stepping out onto his patio, he froze as she stepped out of the guest house. The flowered dress was light and airy, hugging her breasts with a deep V, giving him a view of her cleavage that made his mouth water. When his eyes traveled lower, he realized that her long, sexy legs were revealed with every step she took. The ruffles of her dress shifted, revealing the tanned length of those legs that had only this morning been wrapped around his waist.

This was going to be a long night, he told himself.

"Wow!"

Mack stepped out of the house behind Reid.

"Who is *that*?" he asked.

A soft chuckle came from Brant. Reid should say something, but he was too entranced by the gentle sway of her hips, the look in her eyes that announced to the world that she knew she looked stunning. The look that turned him on unlike anything he'd ever seen before. She was gorgeous and she knew it! What a turn on! A beautiful woman was one thing. But a woman with that kind of confidence? Damn!

"You're going to introduce me, right?" Mack asked hopefully.

Brant shook his head and, out of the corner of his eye, Reid saw Brant put a hand out, stopping Mack from approaching Selena.

"That's Reid's woman," Brant said softly.

There was a stunned silence and Reid knew that Mack was staring in frustration. Then he sighed. "Figures," Mack grumbled. "Who is that then?"

Any other time, Reid would have turned to find out who had drawn Mack's attention now. But Selena was approaching and he couldn't tear his eyes away.

"That's trouble," Brant growled. And then he was gone, probably heading towards the "trouble", but Reid focused on Selena.

Unfortunately, she veered away from him, heading towards the other guests. Probably what he should be doing right now, but he didn't care. He wanted to lift Selena into his arms and carry her off somewhere private. Some place where he could explore that dress.

More guests arrived and the event coordinator approached him, whispering something in his ear. But he had no idea what she'd said, too focused on Selena. He must have responded with something because the coordinator moved away. So did Selena.

Looking around, he was surprised to see so many people. When had everyone arrived? He'd only been standing here for... looking down at his watch, he realized that the party had been going for a half hour. He'd been admiring Selena and her dress for thirty minutes?

With a chuckle, he shook his head and moved into the fray. Grabbing a beer, he joined a group of guests, talking about... something. He had no idea what they were discussing or even if he participated in the conversation. He was focused on Selena, watching her as she moved from one group to another. He could see the tension in her shoulders, knew that she hated events like this, but admired how gracious she appeared. Whoever she spoke with, she made them feel as if they were the center of the world. They smiled and laughed, nodded their heads at everything she said. Selena was a beautiful hostess, he realized.

Someone bumped him from behind and he turned, ready to snap at them for interrupted his enjoyment of Selena's graciousness. But it was Brant and he looked about ready to kill someone. Looking in the direction of his glare, he realized that his brother was glaring at the lively Italian financial guru as she laughed with another man.

"You have it as bad as Reid," Mack said, slapping Brant's back hard enough to topple a regular man. But the Jones brothers were used to rough slaps of "affection" and the gesture didn't even cause Brant to wobble.

"You don't know what you're talking about," Brant growled.

Mack only chuckled and took another long drink of his beer. Reid didn't care what was going on. He simply enjoyed watching Selena. A few more barbs passed between his brothers but he ignored all of it. It occurred to him that Selena was avoiding him. Every few moments, he caught her looking around and several times, she caught his eye only to look away quickly so that she could move in the opposite direction.

Fine! She wanted to avoid a confrontation while the other guests were around? He could handle that. He knew where she would be when everyone else went away. Sitting back, he relaxed in one of the chairs, appearing to be casual as the others ate the barbeque ribs that were being passed around by the waiters. Everyone was having a good time and the party was a resounding success. But Reid wanted them all gone.

Several hours later, the last of the guests waved goodbye. The catering crew were mostly packed up, the food wrapped and stored in his fridge. The flowers had been brought into the house, the vases scattered about the house and Brant and Mack were inside watching some sort of sports event on his basement television. It was a huge area with a massive television surrounded by reclining leather seats – the perfect man cave.

Selena was walking around cleaning up the last bits of the party. She was exhausted, but still looked amazing even though the killer heels she'd donned earlier in the evening had been kicked off to the side, sitting drunkenly in the grass now.

"The cleaning crew is coming back tomorrow to do all of this," he said, the night making his voice seem louder.

"Of course," she snapped and walked over to pick up several napkins that had fallen behind a bush.

"Selena..." her whole body stiffened.

"I'm tired," she announced, leaving the newly retrieved napkins on one of the poolside chairs. "I'm going to sleep."

"We need to talk. I don't know..."

"Not now," she said and held up her hand. "It's been a long day."

"Fine. You're tired, but at least let me..."

She bowed her head and he saw her shoulders trembling. His whole body hurt at the realization that she was so close to tears.

"Selena!" he growled and moved across the stone patio to take her into his arms. She stiffened immediately but he didn't release her, rubbing his hand comfortingly up and down her back. "Talk to me. Tell me what I did wrong. I know that I hurt you, but I honestly don't know how!"

"I'm not..." she stopped when the sobs overwhelmed her. "I'm not a piece of meat!" She ripped out of his arms, but only because Reid was so stunned by her words. "I'm not a piece of meat that you can just..."

"What the hell are you talking about?"

"You and..." she hiccupped, covering her face with her hands. "This morning! You were bragging to your brothers about what a perfect piece of meat I am! I'm not a piece of meat! I'm a human being! I'm a person with feelings and words hurt! You can't just..."

"I never said that!"

She swung around, her teary eyes glaring up at him. "You did! This morning! After I came out of the pool, you were saying to your brothers what beautiful piece of meat I was!"

He stared at her, his mind trying to figure out what she was saying. He'd never referred to a woman in such a callous manner in his life. His sister would have castrated him and all of his brothers if she'd gotten even a whiff of them treating a woman poorly.

"You said I had a perfect rack!" Her hands moved up to cover the cleavage revealed by the gorgeous dress.

Those words struck a memory and he looked at her, shocked by how she'd interpreted his words. "Selena...I was talking about the ribs," he explained gently, knowing that he had to be careful. "You do have beautiful breasts, honey. But when the caterer had arrived this morning, they brought a massive amount of pre-cooked ribs. If you're talking about a conversation I had with my brothers while you were swimming, we were talking about the rack of ribs that the caterer was brushing with more sauce." He moved closer, watching her stunned eyes carefully. "Honey, you have to believe me when I say that I would never talk about any woman like that. Never!"

Her mouth fell open and he touched her, relieved when she didn't shrink away from him.

"You're beautiful, Selena. And yes, you have breasts that make my mouth water, but I'm a leg man. So if there's anything I admire about you most it is your legs." Closer still. "I love your legs. They are strong and sexy and when you wear those heels, I can't even think!"

Still nothing, but he could see that she was thinking.

"The ribs?" she whispered.

Her words came out scratchy and he ached to hold her. So instead of holding back, he pulled her into his arms, tucking her head under his chin as he felt her body tremble against his. "Ribs, honey. Not you." He smiled. "Although, feeling your breasts against my chest right now is pretty nice."

A laugh! She actually laughed! She might have smiled during the party, but this was the first time he'd heard her laugh all day long! It sounded...beautiful.

"Maybe you should tell me what happened in your past, Selena. I suspect that those memories are a bit of a landmine. And..." he hesitated, feeling her body stiffen. He pulled away slightly. "I want you in my life forever, Selena. But I don't want to trigger memories that will hurt you." He took her hands, gently holding her fingers. "Will you tell me what happened in your past, please? Will you explain?"

Ribs? He'd been talking about the ribs? That actually made sense. Thinking back, Selena remembered the caterers. And yes, the ribs had smelled amazing. Not that she'd had any, being too sick to her stomach about what she'd thought Reid had said about her.

But food? He hadn't been talking about her and sharing her with his brothers...?

She looked up at Reid and the truth hit her all at once. She'd been wrong! So incredibly wrong! "I'm sorry!" she whispered, unaware of the tears streaming down her cheeks now. "I'm so sorry!"

"Talk to me, honey. What happened in your past that would cause you to think anyone would say something like that," he urged.

Selena shuddered as the memories hit her. The memories and his tenderness. He was such a raw, powerful man but at the moment, he was...kind. Gentle.

Could she tell him? Could she bring back the memories and say them out loud?

He reached into his pocket and Selena gasped as the ring sparkled in the moonlight.

"I want you Selena," he said softly. "Not just for the weekend or for the week or the next month. I want you forever. I want every part of you." He slid the ring onto her finger and Selena couldn't stop the tears from falling

"Oh Reid," she whispered, wanting to pull her hand away but she kept it still, waiting until the ring was all the way on. "It's beautiful. But..."

"No buts, Selena. Talk to me. Let's build a life together, but tell me about the minefield that is your past."

She covered her mouth, trying to stop another sob, but it was pointless. After this afternoon, she wanted, needed, his arms around her. "You really don't..."

"Never!" he insisted. "I don't think of you like that and I would never think of any woman like that. And when we have kids, our sons will grow to respect women as equals and we'll teach our daughters to kick the butts of any male who doesn't respect them."

Such precious words! So amazing to hear! She couldn't hold back any longer. Throwing herself into his arms, she sobbed against his chest.

His arms closed around her, pulling her in close. "Would you tell me what happened? What someone did to you?"

He felt her stiffen but he only tightened his arms around her, trying to reassure her. "I can't!" she finally whispered.

He pressed a kiss to the top of her head, squeezing her tightly. "I think it is important, Selena."

He carried her over to one of the lounge chairs. The darkness surrounded them and he continued to hold her, waiting for the trembling to subside. Slowly, the shivers stopped and her breathing evened out, but he knew that she hadn't fallen asleep. She might not be shivering, but she was still tense.

"Was it in high school or college?" he prompted, wishing he could find the boys who had done this to her and pummel them.

There was a long silence and he could feel the debate inside of her. "Both," she finally admitted.

His arms tightened again. "What happened in high school? Is that when the anorexia...hit you? Developed? I don't know the right terms to use, I apologize. "

"I developed anorexia in college. I got help before I had to be hospitalized though. So that's something."

"What happened in high school?"

She laughed, a harsh sound. "I was chubby in high school. There wasn't just one thing that happened in high school, it was just a series of small stabs. The cheerleaders mocking me for my weight, running in gym class." She shifted. "I think that gym teachers are evil. They are so athletic, that they don't understand how an unathletic person can fumble around. It's like programming comes pretty naturally to some people. Others are gifted with the ability to read body language and are excellent sales people. Gym teachers are just naturally athletic." She looked up at him. "Some are good teachers and I'm generalizing unfairly. But my high school gym teachers were horrible. They humiliated me when I couldn't run as fast as the others in class. They taunted me in the locker room. They never stopped any of the other girls in class from saying mean things to me." She sighed, pressing her face into his chest. "If a student is bad in English or history and gets a bad score on a test, the student can hide the test score and their failure isn't as public. But in gym class, every failure is right there in the open. The unathletic student has no way to hide. And gym teachers are infamous for just telling people to 'do it' and not actually teaching."

"But you're an excellent runner now. I would never have known that you'd had a problem when you were younger."

Selena smiled, turning her head to kiss his chest before resuming her story. "In college, after...well, after I got help, I found a running coach. This woman was wonderful. She taught me how to run, how to control my breathing, to pace myself. When I was in gym class and we had to run on the track, I was so worried about being the last person in the class to finish, I'd sprint right off of the starting line. This woman showed me to go slow, to find an easy rhythm." She snuggled against him. "I wish I'd learned that earlier. Although, high school gym class was so cruel and the pressure to

185

not be humiliated so intense, I probably would have done the exact same thing."

"I remember the slower people in gym class."

"You weren't one of them, were you?"

He sighed and kissed her head again. "No. I'm sorry Selena. I don't think I ever made rude comments, but I didn't stop the others either."

She was still for a long moment and he thought he might have lost her at that point. But she turned and rubbed her cheek against his chest and he breathed a sigh of relief. "I forgive you."

He hugged her, but then pulled back again. "What about in college?"

Another long silence and he could feel the tension increase in her slender figure once again. He wasn't sure she'd tell him and he would be fine with that. She'd opened up so much tonight. He wouldn't make her tell him everything now. They had a lifetime of telling stories and learning about each other.

Then she shifted, her back against his chest as she stared up at the stars. "A really cute fraternity boy flirted with me. We were in the library at the beginning of my freshman year so I was already nervous and feeling lost. The other girls in school were all skinny, blond, and gorgeous. I was no longer just chubby." She paused again. "I was really heavy. Worse, I refused to get clothes that fit me, so they were tight and uncomfortable. I wore big shirts to hide my size, but what I didn't understand was that those shirts only made me look larger."

"And the guy teased you in the library?"

She shook her head. "Worse. He flirted with me until I agreed to come to a frat party with him that weekend."

Reid wasn't sure he wanted to hear the rest of this story. He could guess where it was going. College freshmen boys were cruel idiots. He could imagine Selena with more weight on her figure.

She was beautiful now, but with more weight, her features would soften, her hips would be rounder. And her legs...he doubted her legs could ever be bad! She had gorgeous legs!

"I bet you were lovely," he whispered into her ear.

"I knew how to put on makeup and do my hair and thought that was good enough."

"Selena, you're beautiful! Inside, you're a gorgeous person. On the outside, you're healthy and vibrant, but inside, you're sweet, caring, and kind."

She smiled, lifting his hand to kiss it. "Thank you for that. But I was insecure and painfully shy."

"I can see that. You're still shy."

She laughed and the sound felt like a sultry caress.

"I thought I hid it well."

He chuckled. "I can see through the bravado."

"Yes, well, this guy played on my shy nature. He manipulated me. I was..." she choked on her next words but Reid waited patiently, ready to listen but bracing himself for whatever she might tell him. "I was his fraternity challenge. He needed to have sex with a big girl in order to meet his initiation goals."

Reid muttered several curses under his breath. When she wiggled slightly, he realized that his arms had tightened around her. He relaxed his grip, but kept her close. "What was his name?" he asked, a threat to his voice.

"Jeremy Kingsley. He was tall and handsome, but prematurely laughing at his conquest of me. I came to the frat party that night, looking for him and all dressed up. I'd curled my hair, my makeup looked perfect and I was wearing my prettiest dress."

He closed his eyes, picturing her in his head. "I'm sure you looked hot!"

She sighed. "I thought so. I'd just grabbed a beer when I heard him talking. He was bragging about winning the frat house contest and having sex with me before any of the other pledges. He'd bragged about how he'd flirted with me in the library and how little effort it had taken him to convince me to come that night."

"Please tell me you kicked his ass."

He felt the drop of wetness fall on his hands and hugged her closer.

"I walked out. I walked back to my dorm room and…didn't eat for three days."

"Selena," he groaned, closing his eyes as her pain washed over him.

"For a long time, I survived on water and about two hundred calories a day. On the days I ate more, I'd beat myself up and the next day, I wouldn't eat anything. Eating was the enemy. Food was bad. My mind twisted everything around. I lost about fifty pounds in two months. Everyone in my dorm told me how much better I looked, which only reinforced the warped thoughts in my mind. It got worse and worse until…"

"What happened?" he prompted.

"I fainted in class. The paramedics were called. Even after they revived me, I couldn't figure out where I was, couldn't give them my name. I hadn't eaten in more than thirty-six hours, so my body wasn't functioning properly. And I'd lost so much body fat, my body had no reserves."

"That's when you realized you had a problem?"

She laughed harshly. "Nope. My parents were called to the hospital. I stayed there for three days while they assessed the damage to my heart and other organs. Thankfully, because my starving was recent, I hadn't done any permanent damage, but I still needed months of therapy. I dropped out of school that semester in order to heal. I fought it for a long time, furious that my parents didn't understand. Finally, the therapist my parents forced me to see showed me pictures of my body taken at the hospital and I saw how thin I'd gotten. It was bad," she whispered. My ribs and hip bones protruded. I was literally skin and bones. Normal body fat percentages are about twenty-five percent for women. I was down to about ten percent which is about as low as a person can go before real damage to the organs starts to happen."

"How long did it take you to recover?"

Selena sighed. "It's ongoing. It is a bit like being an alcoholic. They can't cure the disease. Just as I will always have to be mindful of eating and the messages I tell myself. It's ongoing. Some days I'm strong and other days, I struggle. I know my triggers and I avoid them." She glanced behind her, giving him a small smile. "Bacon is the biggest trigger for me, but I have others."

"We'll never have bacon in the house. Promise."

She smiled, grateful for the immediate support. "I'm pretty good most of the time."

"We all struggle with something in our lives," he told her.

She turned and looked up at him. "What do you struggle with?" she asked, not believing him for a moment.

"I have the most annoying siblings you will ever meet!" he teased. When she laughed, he turned serious. "I have a bad temper. I'll never hurt you, but it is easily sparked by triggers. I'm not as conscious of them, so my temper flares unexpectedly." He pulled her higher. "So how about if we make a deal? I'll help you with your eating and you help me with my temper."

She laughed, knowing that it wasn't the same, but she felt a tenderness inside of her for the offer. "Deal," she told him.

He leaned forward to kiss her and Selena lifted her face, meeting him halfway.

"I love you, Selena. And I promise, I will never treat you with anything other than respect. Even when I'm furious with you."

Another laugh and the last of that tension eased from her

shoulders. "I love you too, Reid. I really do! And I promise to fight my inner demons harder."

He nuzzled her neck. "How about if I become an outside demon for you?" and he nibbled on her earlobe, causing her to yelp and laugh at the same time.

Chapter 18

"Are you ever going to explain why we are here?" Brant asked, following his oldest brother into the bar. They'd flown down to Austin, Texas with only one day's warning. Reid had called him and Mack and said he needed help. They'd both dropped whatever they were doing and got on the flight with their oldest brother.

"I told you, I need to find someone."

Mack chuckled and slapped Brant on his shoulder. "I think I understand," he said, looking around at the patrons at the bar. "You're here for backup," Mack explained to Brant.

Brant shrugged. "I always have his back. And yours. But..."

"And I'm here to make sure he doesn't break the law." At Brant's confusion, Mack shrugged. "Or if he does break the law, I'm here to get him out of jail."

Brant looked from Mack to Reid, sure that his oldest brother would deny the statement. But when Reid just continued searching, Brant nodded his head. "Got it." If Reid was ready to do physical harm to someone, this was serious and he turned serious. Not that he was ever not serious, although, he would argue that he relaxed sometimes. Even if one annoyingly bouncy Italian woman seemed to think he never relaxed. He relaxed. Just not when one of his brothers needed backup. Or when he was working. The woman didn't understand that business was a serious time. Besides, he enjoyed his work. Brant found the challenge of figuring out numbers to be invigorating. And he was damn good at it, so she could just stop telling him to relax! Damn it! She was fifteen hundred miles away and Gianna was still driving him nuts!

"You Jeremey Kingsley?" Reid yelled.

"Here we go," Mack muttered under his breath.

"Yep," Brant agreed, then turned, ready for whatever might happen. He shifted into a fighting stance, quickly assessing the others nearest to the man who turned around, belligerently nodding his head in confirmation that he was the man Reid was looking for.

"Yeah. Who wants to know?"

Reid glared at the shorter man with sandy brown hair and perfectly ironed khaki slacks. Brant glanced at the man's slacks, thinking that at least he didn't iron clothes he was going to wear to a bar.

"You're not going home with this asshole, are you?" Reid asked of the lady. "Trust me, he's definitely not worth your time. He'll use and disrespect you."

The woman didn't seem to be overly impressed with Kingsley, so she shrugged and turned to the man on her other side. The second man glanced behind the pretty blond, realized what was about to happen and whispered in the woman's ear. Immediately, the man put a hand to the small of her back and they moved out of the way.

Kingsley noticed the whole scene and his temper flared. "What the hell! Who do you think you are?"

Reid was ready. He appeared relaxed. But that was all an illusion.

"I'm a friend of someone who endured your pathetic pickup lines. Women don't deserve to be disrespected, Jeremy," Reid announced loudly enough that people started turning to watch the scene. "Women are lovely and strong, too strong for pathetic weakling like you."

The man scoffed and leaned back against the bar. "Right. Women are..."

"Watch it," a woman to his left warned.

Jeremy glanced at the woman disdainfully. "Right. Like I'd hit on someone like *you* anyway."

The woman's boyfriend stood up. The bearded goliath towered over Jeremy by at least a foot. "What did you just say?" the man growled, meaty hands curling into fists. The guy was about six feet, seven inches and had about a hundred pounds on Jeremy.

"Ah hell!" Mack muttered.

Jeremy was too drunk to realize he should just back down. The moron scoffed and shook his head. "Relax, Quasimodo. Your bitch can take the truth."

And that was the end of Jeremy Kingsley. The big guy growled and lashed out. The idiot man went down on the first punch, his head bouncing against the side of the bar and then to the brick floor.

A round of applause erupted a split second later and even the bartender clapped as he reached for the phone to call the paramedics.

Reid looked around, furious that he hadn't gotten to hit the guy himself. "Damn it! That didn't go the way I wanted it to go."

Mack patted his brother's back, shaking his head as he laughed. "Relax, brother mine. As I've had to explain to my town repeatedly over the years, there are better ways to get back at someone than violence." He pulled his badge out of his wallet and hung it on his belt as he lifted his cell phone to contact the local authorities. In a swift conversation, he explained what had happened while searching the guy's pockets for identification.

Mack glanced up at Reid, then over to the big guy who was sitting back down at the bar. A silent message was sent and received. Reid walked over to the big guy and patted him on the back. "Hey, my brother's a sheriff and is taking charge of the scene until the locals swoop in. But you know, there's a bit of confusion right now, so..."

"I'm outta here," the big guy agreed, patting Reid on his shoulder before taking out his wallet to pay for the drinks.

"On me," Reid said.

The other guy stared for a moment, then grinned. "You're welcome." A moment later, the guy and his companion were out the door, but stopped to wave to the bartender before disappearing into the night.

Mack read the information off of the passed-out guy's wallet. "Jeremy Kingsely, who works at Mitrotech, according to this business card."

Brant typed something into his cell phone. In the distance, sirens sounded, indicating that either the paramedics or the police were about to arrive on the scene.

Over the next thirty minutes, Mack took control and explained what he'd seen to the police while the paramedics lifted Jeremy Kingsley up onto a gurney and rolled him out of the bar. Even after speaking to some of the other patrons, the local authorities couldn't get any additional information. Apparently, none of the other bar patrons had seen much on the scene and the case was closed after the police ascertained that an unknown person punched out the victim.

"Let's go," Mack announced, herding both of his brothers out of the bar.

An hour later, the three brothers were on Rembrandt Cosmetics private jet, heading back to Denver.

"Care to explain what this little fieldtrip was about?" Brant asked when the jet was cruising through the air.

"Kingsley hurt Selena back in college."

The other brothers took that at face value.

"Okay, so how about if we do things my way?" Mack suggested, a slow, evil grin forming on his handsome features. "It's *so* much more satisfying."

Reid and Brant both laughed. "You're a scary man," Reid said, but he leaned forward, ready to listen.

Epilogue

"I do!" Selena whispered forcefully, fighting the tears because she didn't want to mess up her makeup.

The minister turned to Reid. "I do," he said almost before the minister finished the vows.

The small group chuckled.

"By the power vested in me by the state of Colorado, I now pronounce you husband and wife," the minister announced.

Applause erupted as Reid pulled Selena in for a kiss that seemed to go on and on.

When he finally lifted his head, Selena leaned into him, needing his strength for a moment in order to recover. "How long until we can be alone?" she whispered.

Reid laughed as he led her back down the aisle. "Not soon enough!"

His baby sister was there and Reid paused to glare at her husband. Not because he disliked Prince Jaffri. He actually liked the guy a lot. But...well, hell, it was just habit now! Jaffri simply laughed and pulled Giselle closer, kissing her neck.

Reid ignored him and accepted his sister's congratulatory hug. Mack and Brant were next and he waited semi-patiently as everyone felt the need to hug his wife. Selena gloried in the attention and he thought she was the most beautiful bride he'd ever seen.

"Patience, big brother," Giselle laughingly warned him. "I've created a wonderful celebration for you!"

196

Reid refrained from groaning, but just barely. "You didn't have to," he told her.

She only grinned. "I know, but you deserve it. I really like Selena by the way."

He turned and found Selena talking with Gianna. And Brant was glaring. Interesting.

"I like her too," Reid replied. Turning to look down at his sister, he asked, "Are you happy? Is he treating you well?"

Giselle turned to find her husband, locating him over at the bar where he was sipping a glass with golden liquid in it. He must have sensed her look because his glass froze midway to his lips and he looked in her direction.

"Incredibly happy," she sighed.

Reid rolled his eyes when Jaffri winked at his wife.

"Stop it," she laughed. "I know that you like him. And he likes you too. So just behave." Turning, she looked over at Selena who was surrounded again. "So...tell me what's going on with Brant and that pretty woman he keeps glaring at over there."

Reid turned and, sure enough, Brant and Mack were talking with Jaffri at the bar, but Brant was barely paying attention. All of his focus was on Gianna.

"I wish I knew," he finally replied.

That's when Selena looked up and all of his attention focused on her. He lifted his hand and she took it so that he could pull her away from the crowd and back into his arms. "Have I mentioned that I love you?"

She smiled up at him, leaning against his chest. "A few times today. But I never tire of hearing the words."

"I love you," he said again. "And you look incredible today."

She leaned up on her toes, kissing him lightly. "I love you too, Reid!"

"Your first wedding present," he handed her an envelope.

"Jeremy Kingsley was recently released from his job. Layoffs," he explained, shaking his head in mock sadness.

Selena blinked, not understanding. But she opened the envelope. There was a picture of Jeremy Kingsley carrying a box out of a building, escorted by a security guard. He looked furious and his face was red with embarrassment as his co-workers gawked on the sidelines.

Selena looked up, shocked at the image. Smiling, she moved closer to Reid. "You didn't have to do that," she told him. But deep down, she loved him even more. "You're amazing," she whispered.

"I love you too."

Excerpt to "The Billionaire's Mysterious Temptress"
Coming January 2019

Author's Note: I received several e-mails from readers after the cover reveal on this series. Many of you hated the original titles. So at the printing of Reid's story, I was still in flux on the titles to each of the brothers' stories. I apologize for the slow change over in this – but wanted you ladies to have input into the names.

Anyway – here is the excerpt. Enjoy!

The soft ping of the elevator's arrival was her only warning.

Even the sounds of footsteps were muted by the thick carpeting on the executive hallway but...she knew. Gianna knew exactly who had just stepped off of that elevator. Not because she could feel him, hear him or even because the scent of his spicy aftershave preceded his presence.

Nope. The only reason she knew who was coming down the hallway was because it was seven fourteen in the morning. At ten minutes past seven every morning, Brant Jones drove his sleek Mercedes into the parking lot. At eleven minutes past seven, he stepped through the doors of the corporate headquarters for Rembrandt Cosmetics. The elevator ride up to the executive floor absorbed the next three minutes.

Gianna knew that she could set her watch to his arrival. Every morning, no deviation from the routine.

Twisting the rubber band around with her fingers, she idly wondered what he would do if she snapped the band across the hallway and...!

NO! No, no, no, no! With horror, she stared at the rubber

band that was now laying innocently on the thick carpet. Right next to a very expensive pair of loafers.

Darn it!

"Bored again, Gianna?"

That deep, gravelly voice did crazy things inside of her. A part of her wanted to figure out how to make the man smile. Another part of her just wanted to piss him off. Unfortunately, those opposing impulses seemed to wage a constant battle inside of her head. And equally unfortunate was the lack of a filter inside her head, which meant that she tended to act on those unwise impulses.

"Um..."

Quickly, she shoved the papers under a stack of files. When she looked up at him, his eyes were hard and angry.

Instantly, his eyes moved from the stack of files then back to her face, his gaze narrowing with suspicion.

"In my office, Gianna," Brant Jones snapped. And those shoes continued down the hallway towards the posh executive offices.

Gianna stood up, giving him a bit of time to move further away from her. No point in creating more naughty, ill-advised temptation in her head, she told herself. And watching the man's broad shoulders...well, the ideas that occurred to her simply weren't professional or appropriate.

Moments later, she stepped into his office and stood there, waiting for...something.

"Close the door," Brant ordered. Gianna considered defying that command. It might be better if there were witnesses to her murder.

Then she looked over at the man's glare and all of those naughty ideas came right back to her. That need to get a reaction out of Brant Jones, to make him feel...something, anything at all, hit her hard. So it was that her hand reached out, their eyes locked. He anticipated her act and dared her to follow through. Wrong thing to do, Gianna thought.

That hand just…flipped the door. Slam!

There! Door closed, she thought with satisfaction. And noise! Goodness the loud noise inside this stuffy office felt liberating!

But as she looked up at the man, she knew once again that he was irritated with her. What was new, she thought with increasing resentment.

Brant didn't say anything for a long moment. He simply stared at her. Like a bug. Like a disgusting bug that was crawling across his immaculate, expensive carpet! His immaculate, noise-silencing carpet! How about a tile floor, she thought as she stood there, waiting for his furious inspection of her to end.

"Why would I install tile?"

Gianna blinked, cringing inwardly. She hadn't meant to say those words out loud. Darn filter! What's the point of having a filter if it didn't work?!

"Um…just…sound." Giving in to her desperation, she moved forward, her hands lifting into the air to implore him to understand. "Don't you ever want some noise? Something to let you know that you're alive and that the world is moving around?" She spun around, sighing as she took in the amazing view of the mountains from his massive office. "Even here in this silent room, it is oppressive! You have a gorgeous view of the Rocky Mountains and yet," her arm swept the air, indicating his desk, "you work with your back to that resplendent view!"

Brant sat down in the leather chair and watched. It was always a delight to watch Gianna with her wild, dark hair that curled all around her lovely, delicate features. Even listening to her was amazing. Her English was brilliant, but the words were tinged with a beautiful, lilting, Italian accent. He almost laughed at her use of "resplendent" but pulled back just in time, not wanting to offend her. He knew that she was constantly pushing to improve her use of the language by trying out different words and phrases. Sometimes her new words were right on target and other times, she...well, didn't. Either way, she was like a shocking breath of fresh air.

Unfortunately, she was bored. He knew that she needed more challenges, more intellectual stimulation, but no matter how many assignments he handed over to her, she finished them with ease and accuracy, wanting more. She was doing the job of three people at the moment. Yet she still didn't have enough work to do.

Still, he couldn't be seen as soft. There was a professionalism within the company that needed to be maintained. "Your father asked me to hire you, Gianna. He wanted you to work, not play games."

She stood up and moved around the office. "I work! But that's all that anyone does around here! They work! No one does anything interesting!" She huffed for a moment, then swung around. "Where is the fun? Where is the laughter? You Americans!" she said with an inelegant snort. "You never do anything fun!"

Brant leaned back in his chair, thinking about all of the fun things he'd like to do with her. Starting with taking off that sexy dress that wrapped around her voluptuous figure. With one, simple tug of that silk tie at her waist, the entire dress would fall open. One tug and he could view all of her lush curves. At twenty-five, Gianna had a very Italian sense of style. The flamboyant colors and simple lines all contributed to the sensuous nature of whatever she wore. Add in her dramatic flair for...everything and it was no wonder Brant was hooked. Completely!

Not that he would do anything about his attraction for Gianna. She was gorgeous and outrageous, flagrantly taunting him some days and others, she just annoyed him by being around him and knowing that he couldn't touch her.

She'd asked him a question. Question? No, she'd made a comment. Something bout...Americans? Yeah, that was it. She thought that Americans were boring and work driven. Oh, if only she could read his mind, she'd know full well that he was focused on her and work...he had no idea what was waiting for him on his desk or on his calendar. On the other hand, Brant was fully aware of the enticing shadow between her breasts and her slender ankles. Pulling his eyes back up to her darker ones, he nodded in agreement. "Yes. Americans are very focused on work issues."

"Why?!" she gasped, once again, dramatically throwing her delicate hands up in the air. "Why can't you just take a day off and..." she gestured toward the mountains. "Just go have a picnic! Luxuriate in the beauty around you! Take a bubble bath or drink some wine!"

"You want me to take a bubble bath?" he teased. Gianna didn't understand that he was teasing her and her disgust escalated. Which only amused him further.

That hand waved in the air in his general direction. "You're such an American! You take everything so actually!"

"Literally," he corrected in what he hoped was a gentle tone.

"Exactly!"

He didn't bother to explain that he was correcting her word usage. Why bother? He actually liked it when she messed up a word or phrase. He thought it was adorable, just like the rest of her.

"So you want to go on a picnic?"

She swung around and he once again had to stifle a laugh when she glared at him. Obviously, his intimidating nature didn't affect her in the same way it affected the rest of his staff. The woman was courageous, he'd give her that much.

"A picnic would be lovely, but it isn't the only thing that would brighten a day!"

He rubbed a finger over his mouth. Damn, he loved it when her accent deepened. He could always gauge her emotions by the intensity of her Italian accent. Right at this moment, she was angry, but even that turned him on.

Ignoring his body's increasing reaction to her lush figure and sparkling, dark eyes, he lifted an eyebrow. "Other suggestions?"

She glared at him, her hands coming to rest on her round hips. "You are mocking me." With a sigh, she looked up at the ceiling, then back at him. Thankfully, he was able to bring his eyes back up to hers before she realized that he was surveying her breasts. Apparently, the dress wasn't made of silk but of some sort of stretchy material because it was literally straining at the seams as the material tried to keep all of her lush curves encased.

"I'm not mocking you Gianna. Your father asked me to take care of you."

Her glare intensified and he wondered what she would do if he lifted her into his arms and...oh, a lot of ideas popped into his mind.

"My father asked you to employ me for this next year."

"And take care of you." He only said that to irritate her further. And yeah, he liked it when she wiggled like that. Brant struggled, and failed, to keep his eyes on her face. But what was a man to do when she moved like that? Did she have any idea of how erotic it looked when she shifted her body in that way? Everything moved! Every sensuous, gorgeous, sexy part of her figure drew his attention! And yeah, his eyes drifted lower, taking it all in. He was only human after all.

"No! No man takes care of me! One takes care of babies and children! I take care of myself! I refuse to allow any man to take care of me!"

He ignored her assertion because Brant had conversed with Gianna's father every week since she'd arrived two months ago. The man was worried about his daughter and demanded updates on her welfare from Brant.

"Are you finished with the report I sent to you yesterday?" he asked.

She shrugged dismissively. "Yes. Your sales are down in the West Coast by two percent but up dramatically in the East Coast," she explained. "Eleven point one percent actually." She swung around to look at him. "The trainer on the east is good. Selena trained that team good and they know how to suggest individual products more better."

Brant leaned back in his chair, enjoying the errors in her language as well as the accent. He listened to Gianna recite specifically which products were more closely aligned with another and lended themselves to upselling. It was an easy, service oriented way of selling more by simply suggesting to the client to purchase mascara remover whenever they came in for mascara. Or suggesting makeup primer when they wanted foundation. It was simple to explain how primer allowed a customer to use less makeup and have it last all day, thereby saving them money in the long term. And Gianna's lilting accent only made the recitation even more interesting.

Gianna, with her brilliant mind and impressive ability to recall even the smallest piece of data, knew the figures for each section of the country and profit margins for each product right off the top of her head. So not only had she done the research, she knew exactly how to improve top-line revenue for the areas that had lower sales. Her analysis wasn't just numbers deep. It was extraordinary!

He needed to promote her. Even if she was only here for the year, the woman's intelligence and insight deserved more responsibility and more money. "So what do you suggest?"

Gianna shrugged. "Get the East Coast trainer out to the West Coast and train the trainers more effectively," she replied as if that were the most obvious answer.

Which it was and he'd already made a note to do that. For the next hour, he snapped out questions for her and she answered them without hesitation and with statistics or data to back up her suggestions. She'd been hired to work in the financial department under Brant's chief financial officer, but the information she provided him was even better than what his CFO, Ken, had provided just yesterday. That man only presented the raw numbers, never the analysis behind those numbers. Ken was good, but Gianna was better. Ken's analysis wasn't as thorough, nor could he spout the data off the top of his head as Gianna could.

Todd, his assistant, knocked on the door, interrupting their conversation that was both enlightening and fascinating.

"What is it?" Brant snapped, ignoring the way Todd cringed slightly.

"I apologize for interrupting, sir, but your first meeting of the morning has convened."

Brant glanced at the computer monitor. Sure enough, there was a flashing message indicating that he was late for his first meeting. Unfortunately, his lack of focus was normal whenever Gianna was around. He knew that he should get back on schedule.

Even so, he focused his attention on the woman sitting in front of him. Her brown eyes flashed defiance as her dark curls danced around her head, her whole body vibrating with energy. What was it about Gianna that made him so...!

The word 'crazy' popped into his mind, but as he studied her dark eyes that dared him to tell her she'd gotten anything wrong during their hour-plus conversation. And damn it, he really wanted to! He wanted to tell her to get the hell out of his office and his company. He wanted to order her back to Italy where her sense of vibrancy and beauty belonged.

Gianna was a complication in his life that he didn't need or want. He absolutely refused to give her enough power over him by admitting that she made him crazy. So what if he looked forward to seeing her every damn morning? And there was no way he'd admit to anyone else that he enjoyed just looking at her, talking with her. Listening to her.

Seeing her smile.

It made absolutely no sense. He didn't trust her, he didn't like her and he definitely didn't think she was beautiful. Even though she was. Stunningly beautiful! And damn, he hated the way her full lips softened, as if she might be thinking about kissing him as often as he thought about kissing her.

Kissing?

Wait. Huh?! What the hell? He never thought about kissing the damn woman! He wanted her gone! Out of his life!

And yet, his eyes dropped to those soft lips again, wondering if she would vibrate with the same kind of energy if he made love to her.

"Sir?"

Brant looked at his assistant, irritated that his concentration on Gianna's lips had been interrupted. "What?"

"Your meeting," The feisty brunette admonished. That's when Gianna stood up and Brant braced himself for the impact of her enticing figure on his body. Gianna was lush in the most lushest of ways. And he blamed Gianna for his lack of mental acuity because she shifted to the left, bending ever so slightly and Brant just sat there watching her, his body tensing for a brief glimpse of her cleavage.

Yeah, he'd been reduced to this, he thought. Brant considered admonishing himself for looking, but Gianna's full, incredibly full, round breasts were…beautiful. And lush. There really was no other way to describe her. Tiny waist, full hips and breasts that would be more than a handful.

She was too short, he told himself. At several inches over six feet, Brant preferred the women in his life to be tall and sultry, with more subtle curves. He liked athletic women, he reminded himself. Looking at Gianna's full breasts, he wondered if she ever played any kind of sports. She had the kind of body men drool over, watch and stare at longingly.

Exactly as he was doing now.

Damn, she was also smart and brilliant and funny. He needed to treat her with respect.

At least until he understood her motives for being here. Why would a woman like Gianna travel halfway around the world to work in Colorado at a cosmetics company? It just didn't make sense.

Printed in Great Britain
by Amazon